Love Rescheduled

USA TODAY BESTSELLING AUTHOR
JENNIFER PEEL

Copyright © 2023 by Jennifer Peel

This book is a work of fiction. The names, characters, places, and incidents are the product of the author's imagination or are used fictitiously. Any resemblance to actual events, business establishments, locales, or persons, living or dead, is entirely coincidental.

All rights reserved. Without limiting the rights under copyright reserved above, no part of this publication may be reproduced, stored in, or introduced into a retrieval system, or transmitted in any form or by any means (electronic, mechanical, photocopying, recording, or otherwise) without prior written permission of the copyright owner. The only exception is brief quotations in printed reviews. The scanning, uploading, and distribution of this book via the internet or via any other means without the permission of the copyright owner is illegal and punishable by law.

Dedication

To all my emotional support extroverts.

A special thank you to Fran Solomita, a fantastic guy and comedian.

One

"Happy New Year, Lord Mac. You were absolutely amazing last night. I daresay you are, without a doubt, one of the best decisions of my life. Well worth the wait." I happily sighed and then ran a finger down the cool, shiny metal of my laptop. I'd been saving for over two years for that royal bad boy. And he was royally bad, as in so, so good. Which was why he'd received a place of honor on the pillow next to me. Also because my reading genre of choice was Regency novels. And if I was going to have a fictitious boyfriend, he was going to be a lord. In reality, Lord Mac ended up on my pillow because I worked way too late last night and I thought it best to rest him carefully and safely next to me. I was a real party animal ringing in the New Year. Like most nights of my life, I was fast asleep by eleven. This may be the reason I nickname my laptops and then sleep with them.

I stretched before sitting up and reached for my phone resting on the nightstand. The sun wasn't even peeking her pretty head up this early in the morning. Most people would probably say I shouldn't be awake, either, given it's a holiday, but I arise at the same time every morning to start my routine. First up, perusing my schedule for the day. Today was special, as I would be going over my yearly calendar items. It gave me a little chill. Why it brought me so much satisfaction, I didn't know.

Probably the same reason I was sleeping with electronics. It was predictable. And there were few things I loved more than schedules and predictability.

I curled my feet under me, enjoying the feel of my silky legs. Yesterday happened to be wax, polish, and shine day. Every Saturday, just like clockwork.

In the glow of my screen, I clicked on my calendar app. A reminder popped up: *Are you ready for September?*

September? Why did I write that note to myself? I thought and thought, trying to remember why I would make such a cryptic note. Nothing came to mind, so I scrolled down to September.

The first week I had scheduled edits for one of my client's new romantic suspense novels. I only hoped this time Holly added some real suspense. I guessed the ending in the first few chapters of her last book.

The rest of September was more of the same: another client and my monthly podcast, *A Party of Two and the Wallflower*, with my best friends. I am the wallflower. Tara and Jolene are the party—always the party. They are, in three words, my emotional support extroverts. If ever I am expected to be at a social function, one or both are required to come with me. Our podcast is all about how to navigate relationships, whether they be romantic partnerships or friendships, between extroverts and introverts. I mostly focus on friendships, seeing as I tend to be found lying with my laptop.

I scrolled all the way through the month until the last day, Saturday the thirtieth. There was one word: *WEDDING*.

Wedding? Whose wedding? How could I forget to note who was getting married? Did I get a save the date? Which isn't a concept I've exactly embraced. Send me the wedding announcement. At which point, I would save the date and then probably not attend unless Tara or Jolene forced me. Although I would be sure to send a lovely gift.

I threw off the covers, feeling unsettled about not knowing

whose wedding I was supposed to be thinking of an excuse to skip. I wasn't usually this careless with my calendar. I looked at the time, knowing full well Tara and Jolene would be sleeping, as they were on Central time in Nashville and I was on Eastern time living in Greer, South Carolina—just named one of the safest places to live, thank you very much. Jolene was part of a big comedy show last night at a downtown club. Tara was a better friend than me and went to support her. I probably would have gone if it were anywhere else except *that* club in Nashville. Sure, I could have hidden in the corner and tried not to make eye contact with anyone. But . . . it's just that club, well . . . it was too much of a reminder of the biggest extrovert to ever infiltrate my life. The *biggest* reason I moved away from Nashville. No time to think about him. I had to figure out whose wedding I'd been invited to in September. The suspense was upending my ordered tranquility.

I bit my lip and decided to wake up my best friends. For all I knew, they hadn't even gone to bed yet. It was completely plausible.

I dialed Tara's number first as she was, let's say, a kinder, gentler soul in the morning. If you spoke to Jolene before her caffeine infusion, it might very well be the last thing you did.

After two rings, Tara answered. "Are you all right? Tell me who died," her voice croaked.

"I'm fine. Why do you think someone died?"

"Because," she yawned. "It's not time for you to call yet."

See, I was predictable. I called Tara and Jolene every day at ten Central. It was perfect, as Jolene was a stand-up comedian by night and a freelance ad copywriter by day, and Tara was a client of mine. She wrote hilarious rom-coms based on her real-life dating experiences. Her latest was a bizarre tale of catfishing. I was pretty sure she was giving up online dating after thinking she had been chatting with a neurologist for three months. That was until she hopped on a plane to Portland ready to go all *Grey's Anatomy* on her Dr. McDreamy only to find out he was in reality a barista at Starbucks. Thankfully, she ended up meeting a nice biology professor while in line waiting for her latte and to confront that liar, Chad. She and the somewhat grumpy professor are still talking. In the book, of course, it's been deemed a love match. We shall see if fiction becomes reality.

"I'm sorry to worry you, but I have a baby-sized dilemma."

"Did the grocery store rearrange the aisles again? We talked about this before. Change can be our friend," she spoke to me like I was five. More like my life coach, Alec, who was helping me to be more spontaneous and less structured. Was it working? After only a year, it was still too early to tell.

"Oh, ha ha. And just for the record, it's ridiculous to move jam to the juice aisle. It clearly belongs with the peanut butter. What other reason is there to buy jam?"

"What about a jam tart?"

"Who has time to make those? And even if you did, you don't need juice."

"That's an astute deduction."

"I feel like you're mocking me now."

"I would never." She laughed a tired laugh. "I'm living off only an hour of sleep. So, if you're not having a jam crisis, what's wrong?"

"I'm sorry I woke you."

"We wish you were here," she said, not in a scolding manner. More like, *We understand you have issues and still love you.* "Jolene killed it last night."

Massive guilt set in, making me squirm. I really needed to be a better friend. "I should have been there, but in my defense, you need your manuscript back. It's brilliant, by the way."

"Thanks, Nat, but I still wish you were here."

"I know," I sighed. "It's just that place." The place where for a moment in time, I thought maybe I could be someone I'm not. Someone who lived life on a whim and in the spotlight. But the glaring rays cast shadows that plunged me into the dark. In that darkness lived the ugly truths of my past and all my self-doubts. It was too much to overcome. I needed order and schedules—a quiet life unhindered by the fame of the man I love.

"Josh . . . ," she hesitated to say his name, though she didn't have to. Josh would always be a part of me, and I made sure to keep up on his life, as hurtful as it was. By keeping up, I meant stalking him on social media anonymously. ". . . Doesn't even live in Nashville now."

He would always live there, at least in my heart. There I would forever keep him.

I steeled myself for what I was about to say. "I'll come to her next show." Alec would be so proud of me. Maybe the life coach thing was working.

"Promise? Like a fairy tale promise where there are dire consequences for breaking your oath. We are talking, sleeping forever until some random guy finds you in the forest and falls madly in love with you and administers the kiss of all kisses."

I laughed at her. She'd been making me swear those oaths since our friendship began back in our college days. It was the first time I truly felt like I had friends. I still wasn't sure why Tara and Jolene claimed me as theirs. I was nothing like my outgoing and adventurous friends, but I would always be grateful that good fortune had smiled down on me.

"I swear a fairy tale promise. Though it doesn't sound too bad to sleep forever, only to be woken up by the kiss of all kisses." Oh, did I miss kissing.

"Are you kidding me? You would freak out if you woke up to some rando kissing you. You'd want to know his medical history and the last time he brushed and flossed."

I pressed my lips together. She was absolutely right. "Fine, I will for sure be there lest some unhygienic creeper kisses me without my consent."

"Now you sound like yourself. So, tell me about your dilemma."

"Maybe *dilemma* is an exaggeration, but um . . . I was going over my yearly calendar and—"

"Of course you would be at this forsaken time in the morning," she laughed.

She knew how bizarrely quirky I was, so her laughing didn't bother me in the least. The fact that she and Jolene still loved me and my idiosyncrasies, after all these years, speaks to how amazing they are.

"I know, I'm a weirdo."

"You're our weirdo." See, they're amazing.

"So, I have a wedding on my calendar for September thirtieth, but I have no idea whose wedding it is. Do you?"

She thought for a moment. "Hmm. I can't think of anyone we know getting married then. When did you type it in your calendar?"

Before clicking on the app to get the details, I put Tara on speaker. I should have thought about doing that first. Maybe it would have jarred my memory. I clicked on the entry. When the info popped up, I let out a little squeak as the painful reminders of that day hit me like a punch to the gut.

"Are you okay?" Tara asked.

"Uh . . . yeah. I remember whose wedding it is now." My throat was slowly closing, making it feel as if I could hardly breathe.

"Don't leave me hanging."

"It's not important. I'm going to delete it."

"No. No. No. Who's getting married?"

"No one."

"Nat, don't make me get mean. Remember, I'm on no sleep *and* you woke me up."

I squeezed my eyes shut. "Fine. It's . . . my wedding," I said as softly as I could, mortified beyond belief.

"What?" she freaked out. "You're getting married? How could you forget that?"

"I'm not getting married."

"Who's getting married?" I heard a groggy Jolene in the background.

"Our best friend," Tara incorrectly filled her in.

"What? She didn't even tell us she was dating anyone."

"I'm not dating anyone."

"Put her on speaker," Jolene demanded in her killer alto voice. I could picture her stumbling into Tara's room in a T-shirt, her wild brunette curls all askew.

"Good morning, darling," I teased.

She wasn't buying it. "What's this about you getting married?"

"I'm not dating anyone. I'm not getting married," I repeated. "It was just a stupid gut reaction two and a half years ago."

"Ohhhh," they said in unison. They were well aware of the circumstances during that fateful time of my life.

Josh had just gotten engaged to his longtime comedic partner who starred in most of his hilarious Instagram and YouTube videos that had catapulted him to fame as one of the most successful stand-up comedians around these days. Josh used to say that he and Camila were just friends, but it only took them five months to get engaged after our breakup. Or I should say, after I broke up with him. Either way, it made me question how friendly they really were. Oddly, they never got married. In fact, Camila was married to someone else now. And yet, the two were still working together. They'd told the press they'd decided they were better off as friends. In the devastation of it all, I scheduled my own wedding, thinking that since I scheduled everything else, why not the eventual ultimate love match? Obviously, I had forgotten that little tidbit until now.

"It's fine. I'm going to delete it."

"You can't do that," Jolene stated. "Isn't it you that says if it's scheduled, it's in stone?"

"Well, yeah, but this is different."

"How?" Tara asked. "Out of the three of us, it's you who wants to be married."

"Odd, considering my history." Let's just say I didn't grow up in the best environment. Not the worst, but it definitely wasn't healthy. But it was true. I wanted to be married and have a family of my own. Even though I knew it would add chaos to my order. Alec and I talked about this frequently in our weekly sessions. We were identifying obstacles and strategies. The first obstacle being that I was doing nothing to meet any eligible men. By eligible, I meant they must meet my well-crafted criteria. Alec wasn't a fan of the criteria.

"I don't think it's strange. You crave stability, and let's face it, you loved being in love."

"Yeah, I did," I quietly admitted. "But obviously I didn't expect my fictitious wedding date to come to fruition. I haven't even dated anyone since Josh."

"Maybe you should call him," Tara suggested. It wasn't the first time she'd said those words.

"No," I was quick to say. "He's moved on and he's happy in LA." A place I could never be happy. Besides, Josh told me if I walked away, there was no coming back. I'd broken his heart . . . and my own . . . but it was better this way. He needed a woman more like Camila, or even my best friends. Someone who was okay with being in the spotlight and the life of the party. If it was true that every party had a pooper, I would be it. Not that I begrudged anyone else having fun at parties. It's just I preferred to sit in a corner and read. Or not go at all.

"Okay, so what's the plan for your September thirtieth wedding?" Jolene asked.

"Seriously, this is so not happening. It was a lapse in judgment brought on by severe emotional anguish."

"Oh no. I don't think so. You never schedule anything unless you mean it. Besides, you really need to get out more," Tara admonished me.

"I was distraught," I half-whined. It was all coming back to me. When I'd seen Josh's engagement announcement on that Instagram post on his thirty-first birthday, I immediately made plans for my wedding. I chose that date because it was right before I turned thirty. And for whatever reason, I wanted to be married before I started the next decade. And I had thought a fall wedding with only a few people in the backyard of the tiny cottage my beloved nana left me, which I now call home, would be perfect.

"Be that as it may, you always keep to your schedule. This is so happening." Jolene sounded way too giddy, considering it was an adjective I wouldn't have previously used to describe her.

"This is ridiculous. You just don't schedule love." Sure, in a moment of deep despair I thought I could, but no one should hold me accountable for that now.

"If anyone can, it's you." Tara deadpanned.

That was kind of true. I had a knack for making everything on my schedule work out. But love? That was going to take some major planning and probably extra sessions with Alec. The only time I'd ever been in love, it had caught me by complete surprise. No planning involved on any level. That's how I ended up with my polar opposite—Josh. He hated schedules and left his underwear on the floor. Worse, he didn't wash his jeans in between wearing them. Don't even get me going on how often he washed his towels. Or should I say how infrequently? And his place always smelled like old Chinese takeout. But I loved him despite us constantly driving each other crazy.

"I'm picking out my maid of honor dress," Jolene chuckled.

"Hey, I'm going to be her maid of honor," Tara complained.

I smiled even though this was insane talk. "You can both be the maid of honor in my fictitious wedding."

"No ma'am," Tara's southern side came out. "We expect your wedding plan by tomorrow."

"We know how you love to make a good plan," Jolene added. "This better be your best one yet. Talk to you soon."

They hung up, leaving me staring at my phone, crazy thoughts consuming me. Could I really schedule love?

two

AT EXACTLY 10:00 A.M., I walked out the door into the chilly morning, ready for my daily walk around the nearby city park. I made exceptions for rain and the rare times it snowed. The exception was for location only, as my walk was nonnegotiable. Thank goodness for my treadmill. And in the summers, I walked earlier because of the heat and humidity. One could say I was a creature of habit and comfort. Alec would say I was a creature who lived in the comfort zone. He didn't say it to be callous. He knew I didn't grow up in the kindest of situations and I had some pretty embarrassing things from my past that scarred me. Think public humiliations and selfish parents who made me feel ultra-self-conscious. So, he understood my need to control my environment. Was it the healthiest? No. But was I working on it? Uh . . . slowly. Maybe tomorrow I would leave at 10:01. Maybe.

I took in a deep breath of the invigorating air while looking around at the old neighborhood, the place I had felt the most secure throughout my life. Well . . . perhaps Josh's arms won that honor. Unfortunately, he was, in general, way out of my comfort zone. It was fine. He had moved on and I . . . well, I was reconciled to the fact that we were incompatible. He would probably be in bed for another six hours, sleeping on unwashed sheets. And when he rolled out of bed, he would throw on jeans he'd previously worn at least three times.

A vision of a shirtless Josh wearing only jeans popped into my head. I squeezed my eyes shut as if that would help put out the flames of desire roaring inside as I thought of how amazing it felt to lay my head in the softness of the chest hair covering his defined pectorals. I loved the way his fingers would dance down my arm as he spoke about how lucky he was to have me in his life.

I ran a hand through my red pixie-styled hair, making myself think of his kitchen and living room stacked with a disgusting number of takeout boxes and crusty dirty dishes. Then his fans accosting him everywhere we went. Especially the female variety. Anything to remember all the reasons it hadn't worked between us and never would.

I walked down the brick porch steps, remembering time spent on them with Nana snapping green beans. She was from a forgotten generation of women who grew sizable gardens and canned anything they could. She was a penny pincher extraordinaire and would say things like, "You can never get enough of what you don't need." Yet, when she was able, she always did what she could for me, whether it was a new pair of shoes or a book. Mostly, she just loved me for who I was. And she gave me probably the best and possibly the worst advice of my life. She would say, "Natalie, most things in life are out of your control, but you can always control your emotions and how you respond to any situation that arises." Boy, had I ever taken that advice to heart. I was sure she hadn't meant for me to become a control freak, for lack of a better phrase. But when you had parents like mine who obviously didn't care to be raising a child and believed children should be seen but not heard, you coped by learning how to be invisible. I became so good at it, that's where I felt the most comfortable. I did anything I could not to be noticed by people. It didn't help that when people did notice me, it was for something horribly embarrassing. Like the time I thought maybe if I did something amazing, my parents might actually be proud of me and love me, so I entered my junior high's talent contest. You heard that right.

Have you ever seen the movie *About a Boy*? Unfortunately, that poor kid's experience mirrored my own, except I didn't have a Hugh Grant type to jump up on the stage and save me. Perhaps the kids at my school weren't as awful as the ones in the movie. No booing, but there was a lot of laughter. Regardless, it was an unmitigated disaster. I forgot half the lyrics to "What a Wonderful World" and my voice squeaked. I'd begged my parents to come. They walked out before I even sat down. It was a good thing we moved a lot, given that my parents found it difficult to maintain steady employment. Needless to say, I never sang in public again. I even have a hard time singing in the car or shower when I'm completely alone. I made an exception when Nana was about to pass on to the next life. She'd requested I sing "Amazing Grace" at her bedside as I held her hand, silently begging her not to leave me. Josh was by my side, holding my other hand and wiping away my tears.

I had to stop thinking about him and my past. At the very least, I shouldn't let it rule my life, but somehow it always manifested itself.

Alec would tell me right now I needed to remember all my successes in life. I guess the fact I didn't turn into a total psycho, given my upbringing, is a win. This morning I had more pressing matters at hand. My best friends were going to try to hold me to my schedule. Granted, I hated to not keep to my calendar, but I wasn't sure how I was supposed to get married in nine months. I really should have set a reminder sooner. It surprised me I hadn't. In my defense, I was distraught when I came up with the ridiculous idea of scheduling my wedding without even a prospective groom on the horizon. That horizon was still barren. Alec had been giving me some great dating advice lately. His latest tidbit was to tell me to look at dating like reading a book. It would give me the opportunity to picture another version of my life. If I liked what I saw, I could keep reading. If not, I could put the book back on the shelf. It sounded simple enough. I supposed if I wanted to have a wedding, I should probably go to a figurative bookstore.

I hit the paver stone path leading to the sidewalk, thinking about different bookstores. A few weeks ago, Alec had suggested I let my friends set me up. I wasn't sure that was a good idea. They had played a part in Josh and I getting together. Tara and Jolene had dragged me to an after-party where I had mostly sat in a corner and read while they did their thing. I'd noticed Josh kept walking by—once he'd even stopped with a random book and sat next to me, pretending to read. He never said a word, but admittedly, I kept finding my gaze drifting his way. There was something about his soulful chocolate-brown eyes, his mussed dark hair, and his crooked smile, complete with dimples, that I found appealing. I'd tried not to be attracted to him as I'd watched him onstage earlier that night, making the crowd roar with laughter. I knew then he would headline shows. After I'd basically ignored him, he'd gotten my friends involved.

It took a month of them trying to convince me to go on a date with him, coupled with Josh sliding into my DMs to send me memes he'd made highlighting "the wonders of Josh," as he'd called them. I'd finally relented, against my better judgment. By then, he was already semi-famous. I'd thought I would go out with him once and he would see how boring and weird I was and it would put an end to it all. Instead, we ended up talking all night and then eating breakfast together at some dive. After that, we were pretty much inseparable. I smiled to myself as I walked toward the park, thinking of how annoyingly adorable he had been and surely still was.

But then he started touring a lot. The long stretches apart and his ever-increasing fame put a strain on our relationship. I tried life on the road with him, but a tour bus just wasn't for me. There was no being invisible and no routine. At all. And it reminded me of growing up, always moving, never having a place to call my own for any extended amount of time. Worse, everyone expected me to be a certain way because I was with Josh. When they found out I wasn't, I could see the looks and hear the whispers. People wondered why Josh was with someone as boring and awkward as me. All it made me want to do was disappear into the wall. Meanwhile, Josh lived for the next city and stage, as he should. He was amazing and people loved him. But I couldn't live like that, and knowing I was miserable made him miserable, so when Nana passed away and left me her home, I broke up with him and moved to Greer.

I really, really needed to stop thinking about it—him. I'd made the right decision. More than anything in this world, I wanted Josh to be happy. Judging by all the clips and videos I'd seen of him on social media, when I let myself stalk him for twenty minutes once a week on Fridays and on his birthday, he seemed more than happy. Mission accomplished. Now it was time for me to think of my happiness and future. Could that include getting married in nine months? It would definitely be out of my comfort zone. Honestly, the fact I hadn't completely ruled it out was giving me heart palpitations. Alec better give me a figurative star on my chart just for considering it.

While I contemplated this bizarre possible plot twist, I waved at a few people driving by in the quiet morning. I wasn't completely socially awkward, just mostly. In fact, I loved a good polite wave. There was something stabilizing about it. It said I was at home and safe. It's all I ever wanted in this world.

I crossed under the arched entrance of the park, which still donned a Christmas wreath, to find I was very much alone on this sleepy holiday morning. Not even Hal and Stu had arrived to cheer me on. They were the most adorable old men on the planet—friends and neighbors for over sixty years—and part of my routine. Each morning I walked, they would shuffle over and sit on a park bench, shooting the bull, as they called it. Periodically, they would shout out positive affirmations as I walked around the path that wove through the park. I called them my cheering section. Everyone needed one. Hal and Stu were right up there with Tara and Jolene.

If only I could converse with men my age as easily as I did with my two senior citizens, I might have a shot at scheduling love. I still wasn't sold on the insane idea, as intriguing as it appeared. Though I would admit to loving the thought of finding my forever someone. Or, you know, finding him again, except this time he would be just a normal, everyday guy who went to work and came home every night at the same time. That way, we could eat dinner promptly at six while we chatted about our day. Then we would snuggle on the couch and watch a show. This would be followed by an hour of sexy time before my nightly facial and stretching routine. Finally, it would be time for bed. It was perfect. Not to say I wasn't willing to negotiate on times and frequency, even on my routine. I knew things would have to be more give and take. And I was trying to be more flexible. Just last week I'd flown to Nashville on the worst day ever to fly—Christmas Eve—so I could spend the holiday with my best friends. Don't even get me going on how crowded and not on time the flight was.

Did I stay for New Year's? Obviously not. I could only take so many nonroutine things at a time. And I knew they would have convinced me to go to *that* comedy club with them. I wasn't sure my heart could take it. Or risk potentially running into people who knew and loved Josh, which was basically everyone. He was a Nashville legend. And I was the woman who had broken his heart. Or so the rumor goes. Like I said, he'd moved on awfully fast with the gorgeous and talented Camila. Their fans loved it. They had been wanting to "ship" them since the first video they'd released about how ridiculous proposals had gotten.

"There's Hepburn," Hal thankfully saved me from my thoughts. It never went well for me once I got on board the Camila and Josh train. It was best to leave well enough alone.

I turned to find my two favorite old men shuffling my way, each wearing a winter jacket and bow tie. I loved that they called me *Hepburn*, even though I didn't feel worthy of the nickname. They said I reminded them of the ever lovely and timeless Audrey Hepburn, except I had red hair and light green eyes. Somehow, I had fooled Hal and Stu into thinking I was charming and beautiful. They obviously hadn't seen me on a date or when I was a teenager.

I walked their way and met them at their usual bench. They carefully lowered themselves to sit to a symphony of snaps, crackles, and pops. I admired the men who had defied the ugly prejudices and racism of their time to become and stay friends. They met playing in a jazz band. Later, they opened a grocery store together and raised their families side by side. They'd even marched the streets in solidarity, with the hope that their children would have more opportunities and a better way of life.

"Happy New Year," I greeted them.

"How's our girl doing?" Stu asked, holding his curled fingers out to me.

I took his hand and gave it a little squeeze. There was something so comforting about it. He once admitted to having a crush on my nana before he'd met his wife. I wished Nana would have married him. I never met my grandpa, as he died before I was born, but from what I had gleaned over the years from Nana and my father, he wasn't the best man. My father carried a great deal of resentment toward him. Though I think he turned out to be much the same way as him, cold and selfish. My poor Nana.

"I'm doing well," I sighed.

Hal narrowed his dark eyes full of warmth and wisdom at me. "I think you're not telling the full truth, young lady."

I bit my lip. "Well, there is a little something," I admitted.

"Tell us all about it and we'll fix it." Stu chuckled.

"If only you could." I thought it best not to mention what my little—or big—something was, depending on how you looked at it. It's not that Hal and Stu didn't already know how odd I was. Anyone who knew me was well aware of how neatly I organized my life. No need to make them think I was even odder. Besides, I would probably delete the wedding date from my calendar.

I rubbed my chest. That thought pricked me more than I thought it would. Maybe I should keep the date? Maybe? It was going to take some planning. Like, the most carefully thought out, meticulous plan of my life. Of course, it all hinged on finding the right guy. Perhaps Hal and Stu could help me with that part, at least. You know, if I kept the date. And it didn't sound crazy to ask if they knew any available, stable, loyal, non-substance-abusing, well-employed, not-famous men who could pass a background check.

I let out a deep breath and shoved my hands into my fleece jacket pockets. "Um . . . well, maybe you could help with a little something. Do you know any single guys? We are talking cream-of-the-crop kind of men."

Hal and Stu's brows jetted upward, crinkling their almost bald heads.

"Are you looking for love, darlin'?" Stu asked.

I looked down at my cute walking shoes. "Maybe."

Hal scrubbed a hand over his face. "Is this like a New Year's resolution?"

"Something like that."

Stu tilted his head. "Not sure there's a fella good enough for you, but we could start holding some interviews."

"Interviews?" I laughed.

Hal nodded. "I like it. How fast do you need this cream-of-the-crop young man?"

"Well . . . uh . . . I'm just thinking that maybe I should start dating again." I felt like I might hyperventilate. This was becoming a little more real than I had expected.

"You still hung up on that old beau of yours?" Stu asked.

I had mentioned Josh a while back after the guys had asked me if there was a special someone in my life. Josh was special. He had even visited Greer a few times. Nana loved him. Everyone loved him. That was part of the problem.

"No," I responded. Just because you loved someone didn't mean you were hung up on them. I was smart enough to know Josh needed to go back on the hanger. We weren't the right fit for each other. He deserved to be tried on by a woman who was more his style.

The guys narrowed their eyes, judging the truth of my words. I was in earnest.

Hal clapped his hands together and rubbed them. "Sounds like we should get to work. What kind of man are you looking for?"

Oh, I had a list. A long, long list.

three

"YOU'RE HONESTLY CONSIDERING THIS?" ALEC'S deep-brown eyes popped on Lord Mac's screen.

It was our weekly session. Every Monday at 1:00 p.m. sharp. I had just filled him in on my scheduled "wedding date." And the beginnings of a plan that needed a lot of fine-tuning. It basically boiled down to me using Hal and Stu to curate a list of men to interview before setting me up.

I sat up straight at my kitchen table. "Possibly." I squinted.

"Off the record, I have to say: I'm shocked." He used that phrase with me a lot—*off the record*. It meant he was giving his personal opinion versus his professional one. I think he thought of me as a "special" client. And not the way I thought Josh was special.

"So, what do you think on and off the record?" I dared to ask.

"Which answer would you like first?"

"Since I'm paying you a hundred dollars an hour, let's go the professional route."

He gave me his dazzling smirk. I swore he used teeth whitener like it was going out of style. "I do appreciate your patronage. And as your life coach, I think it's great that you have a goal. Especially one that relates to dating again, since that has been the focus of many, *many*," he exaggerated, "of our sessions. It's a positive step forward."

"So, what's your personal opinion?"

"Girl, you're crazy. I love you, but you're crazy. Nobody schedules love." He pursed his lips. "But . . . this is you."

"You make it sound like that's a bad thing."

"You know I adore your quirks. Off the record, of course. What I'm saying is, if anyone could pull it off, it's you."

"That's what Tara and Jolene said." He knew all about them, too. He listened to our podcast. I think for further insight. And of course, I had talked about them frequently. They were really the only family I had now. Well, them and Hal and Stu.

"At the very least, it might help you wade back into the dating pool like you've wanted."

"Or I might drown in the deep end." I'd hardly slept last night thinking of all the potential real-life nightmares that could occur if I embraced this admittedly ridiculous idea of scheduling a wedding without a groom. Like, what if suddenly my date wanted to be spontaneous and changed our plans? And I had no idea what was on the menu at the new place he was taking me to and I ordered something with poppyseeds and several of them got stuck in my teeth? What if he wanted to do karaoke? Or I found out over dinner he didn't believe in properly washing fruits and vegetables before he ate them? How could I let that man be the father of my children? I could hear Josh saying, *"That's what you would be there for."* Oh yes, we had talked about marriage and having children together one day. When you date for two years, those things are bound to come up. Once upon a time, I even believed we could make it work. Which brings me to what really scares me. I know I'm going to have to make solid changes in my life. Not like the kind being with Josh would require, but definitely some. Like I should learn to be more accepting of others' spontaneity. Or maybe even of the fact that my future husband might not believe in cleaning as you go while cooking. Or worse, might not do the dishes before he went to bed. I could possibly wake up to a dirty kitchen. Maybe?

"What have we talked about before? You have plenty of anchors and flotation devices at your disposal. Let's list them," he challenged me.

We had done this exercise probably a dozen times. But it was a friendly reminder. I smiled at a waiting Alec, who looked quite dashing in a pink button-up. It went well with his smooth black skin. He was probably one of the most beautiful humans I had ever met. Don't get me wrong—I wasn't romantically attracted to him. The man knew too many of my neurotic tendencies. Although so did Josh and he still loved me—well, he used to. But I wasn't thinking about him. Except I was totally thinking about him more than I had in a long time. I really needed to stop doing that.

"My first anchor is myself. I'm in control of my destiny. I can also eliminate excuses for why I can't do something." That thought struck me so much, I gasped.

Alec dropped the pen he was using to jot down notes about our session, a sneaky smile on his face. "Did something illuminate you?"

I swallowed hard, a bit freaked out by how much the thought resonated with me. "Well . . . if I really want to find love and be married before I turn thirty, I need to stop generating excuses for why I can't and focus on how I can."

"Very good. I'm putting a figurative star on your chart."

I rolled my eyes, even though I secretly loved the fake stars and chart. "Alec, is this *too* crazy?"

"Only you can answer that. Remember when we talked about your ego and that it's shaped by the very first voices in your life?"

"Yeah," I murmured, thinking of that poignant conversation I had recounted many times. For good and bad, my parents' voices lived in my head. On one hand, they had driven me to be better, as I refused to be anything like them. I did everything I could to get a college education and live a steady life. On the other hand, they had crippled me and brought me to my knees. Even now I could hear them calling me "Fatty" as I went through my chubby adolescent phase before I'd thinned out. Or "Bucky" because of the teeth I had spent a fortune to fix as soon as I was old enough to get a solid paying job. And I had gone to therapy to learn to love my body, mostly. Now I could recognize their manipulations and harsh words were caused by their own exposure to mental and emotional abuse, which stunted their maturity. Despite those things, I still exercised religiously and was super careful about what I ate because I hadn't rid myself of those nagging voices. I never wanted to be that awkward girl again. But I also wanted to hug that girl as fiercely as I could and love her until she embraced all the awkwardness. Until she didn't feel the need to hide from the world.

"Natalie, for you, unfortunately, that voice is your parents, who, let's be real, had no right raising a child." That was the truth. "They led you to believe you were always less, always undeserving. You need to work on becoming the voice you hear."

"I'm trying."

"I know. If your voice is telling you this is something you should do, then I would listen to it."

"Even though off the record you think it's crazy?"

"Listen, some of the greatest accomplishments in the world started with a crazy idea. Maybe this is what you need to help you become the Natalie you want to be. Not to say you need a partner to accomplish that. Honestly, you may not make it down the aisle before you're thirty. But you may learn a lot about yourself chasing this dream with all your heart. Perhaps you'll even find some ways to let go. Maybe, just maybe, you'll discover you deserve all the happiness you've envisioned for yourself."

That was a lovely, lovely thought.

I let out a long breath. "So, I'm doing this?"

"Is that a question or a statement?"

I paused for a moment, blocking out all the reasons I couldn't do this. Maybe even shouldn't. But something deep inside told me to go for it. Be the Natalie I wanted to be. The truth is, I wanted to be in love again and share my life with someone besides Lord Mac. He was so cold in the mornings. I wanted a warm body to wake up next to, with a gravelly voice that spoke of how lucky he was to open his eyes and see me first thing in the morning. I wanted someone to challenge me, like Tara and Jolene do when I get too rigid in my way of thinking and doing things. The only way to accomplish that was to dive right into the water. My shoreline would be September thirtieth. I was wickedly good at making my schedules work out. Why not this one?

I looked Alec straight in the eye. "I'm doing this."

"I can't believe you are really doing this," Tara said. "I mean, I think it's great, but I can't believe it."

"You and me both, but you know how I loathe to cancel anything on my schedule," I half teased. Canceling events really caused me angst. With that said, I was calling her out of the blue, which I hardly ever did. But I thought she and Jolene should be the first to know. And I figured I better tell them so I could hold myself accountable to them. Tara was first to know because Jolene was on a call with her agent.

"You're hilarious," she quipped. "So, what's your plan?"

"Well, Hal and Stu are working on some local prospects for me. I gave them a list of requirements."

Tara snorted. "Let me guess: it's alphabetized and ranked in order of importance."

I cleared my throat. "Maybe. This is important stuff here. Like, the most important decision of my life."

"And here I thought it was whether I should wear bikini or brief undies," she teased me.

"Oh, ha ha. But hipster is the way to go. A little more coverage than the bikini cut, but just as comfortable as the briefs."

"Huh. Looks like I need to go undie shopping. After you tell me what brought on this burst of empowerment."

I pulled my knees up to my chest and snuggled more into the corner of my couch. "I'm tired of being alone. But mostly I'm done being exhausted by battling the fear of being myself. Does that make sense?"

"I think so."

"It's like I have this someone inside me desperate to get out and see what she can do if I would just let her."

"I've met that girl a few times. I like her; she's a lot of fun. But you know I will always love you, no matter who you are."

My eyes stung for how lucky I felt to have such wonderful friends in my life. I may not have many, but the ones I have are golden. "Thank you."

"Well, I think we should get this party started. Should we plan a road trip and go wedding dress shopping?"

"Whoa, whoa, whoa. I think we, I mean I, should probably go on a few dates before we hit up a bridal shop."

"Oh, fine. But think about it. It could be an incentive if you saw a gorgeous dress that cost a fortune in your closet."

I laughed. "That's true, but people would really think I was crazy if I picked out a wedding dress without a groom in sight."

"Uh . . . ," she hesitated. "I'm just going to throw this out there, but since you're being all 'hear me roar' right now, do you think maybe you should call Josh?"

"No," I was quick to say. "Number one on my list is he can't be famous, and he must be home more than away. Besides, you know what Josh said to me." I could still hear the words distinctly in my head: "If you walk out that door, there is no coming back. We're done." Sobbing, I had walked out the door and looked back. I stood in the hall of his complex and stared at that door, begging myself to walk back through it, to be someone I wasn't. In the end, I realized it wouldn't be good for either of us. And I thought maybe if he didn't mean what he said, he would have opened the door and come after me. That doorknob never twisted.

"I know. I just always got the feeling he regretted it."

"He moved on awfully fast."

"I think he regretted that, too."

"Are you still talking to him?" I had to wonder. Not like I would forbid it or even be upset by it. Tara and Jolene loved Josh like everyone else. Not only that, but Josh had helped Jolene catch a big break at the best comedy club in Nashville, Laugh on Tap. Josh had convinced the owner to give Jolene a shot and let her open for him a few years back.

"Not since Jolene and I ran into him last year when he was visiting his folks here."

"Then where is all this 'talk to Josh' stuff coming from lately?"

"I don't know, Nat. I just think there might be some unfinished business between the both of you. And let's be honest, you guys were good together. You had the whole yin and yang thing going."

"Polar opposites."

"Yes, but also connected forces. There can be magic in opposites."

"What are you saying?" I flinched. "I made a mistake?"

"I'm not saying that. I know how hard Josh's life was for you. It would be for a lot of women. And I definitely don't see you living in LA. That wouldn't be good for you. It's just that you're still in love with him. That has to mean something."

"It does. It means I loved him enough to let him go so he could live his dreams."

"It was very noble of you. I mean that. But are you sure your feelings for him won't impede your new adventure?"

I rubbed the back of my neck. "Why would they?" I stuttered out.

"It's just something to think about. It's the way my romance-writer brain thinks. True love never dies, you know?"

"It's not supposed to. If it did, it wouldn't be true. But people can have more than one true love, right?" I was praying the answer was yes or all of this was a moot point, because I would always love Josh.

She didn't answer right away, making me nervous. Like heart palpitations and sweaty upper lip kind of nervous. "Tara," I squeaked out into the silence.

"I think it's possible," she reluctantly agreed.

"Are you just saying that?"

"No. But . . . I have to say, a love like yours and Josh's . . . well . . . I'm not sure that comes around more than once."

Ouch. How was it that the truth can hurt more than lies? But she was right. Josh and I had had something special. At least for a while. I wasn't sure what it was, but it was, in a word, magical. Until it wasn't. "We argued a lot," I reminded her, and myself. Not only that, his lifestyle constantly had me feeling like I was going to crawl out of my skin. That was no way to live.

"Like most couples do."

"But it was about big things."

"That sounds about right." She would know better than anyone. She made it her job to date as many people as possible . . . and then write about them. Some of her exes called her the Taylor Swift of the literary world. That was a huge mistake, as she would only use more of their defects in her next novel. As her editor, I quite enjoyed it.

"So, I just give up?" I was feeling less and less like taking on the world.

"Please don't take it that way. I'm just worried the reason you haven't dated anyone since Josh is because you never really closed that door."

Oh, but I had closed the door . . . and then stared at it. "It's shut tight. I promise." Josh had bolted it, and I wasn't foolish enough to believe it would ever open again. Or that I should even knock on it. I was hit with flashes of the way his features twisted in what I could only describe as pure anguish and shock, my ultimate betrayal reflecting in his eyes, as I eked out, "I will always love you. Goodbye," before turning and leaving. That moment would live with me forever. I knew Josh would never believe it, but my heart was in the right place.

"Okay. If you say so."

Before I could respond, a jubilant Jolene's voice rent the air on the other end of the phone. "I can't believe this is happening!" she shouted.

"What's going on?" Tara asked.

"Put Nat on speaker," she cheerfully demanded.

Tara did as she was told.

"Ladies, you are looking at, or listening to, the next headliner at Laugh on Tap!" Jolene squealed.

I'd never heard her do that before. She actually made fun of people who squealed. It spoke to the significance of her announcement.

"That's amazing," I gushed. "I'm so proud of you. How did this happen and when?"

"Chase Olson was on the schedule to perform this weekend, but the douche has a severe case of laryngitis." It was a well-known fact in the Nashville comic scene that Chase was a pig. His life goal was to sleep with as many women from each of his audiences as he could. Unfortunately, he had talent and was good looking, so he got his wish on the regular. "Mikey"—he was the owner of the club—"just called Geena"—Jolene's agent—"and asked if I wanted to fill in. Of course I said yes." She'd been dreaming of being more than the opening act for years.

"Eep!" Tara shouted. "You have to come, Nat."

I swallowed hard. *You promised you would be a better friend and next time you would go. This is an enormous deal for Jolene.* I knew that. It's just *that* place. So many memories, good and bad. But mostly good. "I'll be there," I said shakily. It's not like I would see Josh there. At least not in the flesh. Maybe it would even help me move on from the past. All I knew was Alec would give me several figurative stars on my chart for this.

four

"PLEASE SLOW DOWN," I BEGGED Tara as we screamed down the highway toward Nashville. My flight had, of course, been late. I swear something in the universe was out to get me and my schedule-loving ways. It was definitely testing my patience. My flight was scheduled to arrive early this afternoon, giving us plenty of time to get to the comedy club, maybe even have an early dinner before we helped Jolene get ready. Now, as it stood, we were barely going to make it in time.

I'd offered to take an Uber even though I'd made a blood oath to never, one, get in a stranger's car, and two, let some random person drive me around. I didn't even like it when people I loved chauffeured me. Not surprisingly, I liked to be in the driver's seat. How could I let someone else be in control of my life? Josh had accused me of being the biggest backseat driver to ever exist. It wasn't my fault he was constantly driving too close to other cars or barely stopping at stop signs. Or worse, he looked at his phone while driving. It was one of our many arguments.

Knowing all this, Tara and Jolene thought it best if Tara just picked me up, lest I changed my mind and didn't come. I probably should have just driven the five hours. But the weather this time of year was unpredictable. The last thing I needed was to get caught in a snowstorm. Perhaps I should have taken my chances, considering I might die due to my best friend's propensity to drive like Mario Andretti with I-65 serving as a speedway.

"No can do. We can't be late." Tara floored it.

I gripped my seat and closed my eyes, repeating in my head a list of things I could control. The only thing I could think of was that I could keep my terror-filled screams to myself. One positive side effect was that the fear made it nearly impossible to think about what I was actually doing. I was entering Josh's turf. The turf we frequented when we were together. Laugh on Tap booked Josh whenever they could, as his shows always sold out. All week I had been thinking about all the women who had fawned over him, slipping him their number. Some even had the audacity to kiss him or grab his butt like he was a piece of meat. It was the same at every venue around the country. Everyone wanted a piece of Josh.

Then there was the after scene, where Josh was, deservedly, the center of attention. I always hung back, not because Josh wanted me to, but because I needed to. As a major introvert, just going to Josh's shows drained all my energy. It got to the point where I wouldn't even go to the after-parties or dinner. I even stopped going on the road with him. Now here I was back in our old stomping grounds, only to be spared by a potential spectacular death on the highway.

"It's going to be fine," Tara tried to calm my nerves.

"If you say so." I peeked an eye open and watched as we whizzed by several cars, their headlights fading into the distance.

"I'm honestly shocked you came."

I turned to face my beautiful friend, her chestnut hair curled and spilling over her shoulders while she gripped the steering wheel, turning it erratically. "I promised I would."

"You did, but I know this isn't easy for you."

"I did an extra session with Alec," I admitted. He'd helped me visualize my visit and come up with strategies to make Jolene the focus of the night, not my need to be invisible or in control. We did gratitude exercises to help with any negative thought processes that might creep up. Thoughts like I would never be good enough for Josh—or anyone, for that matter. It was ridiculous the amount of energy I had to muster to support my best friend. I just hoped no one from the "old" crowd engaged me in conversation. I was sure they all hated me, anyway. Besides, they were mostly all team Camila, like the rest of the world. But the world didn't know what we had. They never would.

Tara chortled. "There's no shame in that. I'm just happy you're here. We miss you."

"I miss you both, too." Being away from them was the one downside of Greer. Although Greer was much more my pace, I missed them every day. When I lived in Nashville, I had chosen not to share an apartment with them. I figured it was better for everyone that way. Not to say they were slobs like Josh, but being such a creature of habit can be hard on other people. No need to push away my genuine family. "By the way, if I die tonight, please let my date for next week know why I literally ghosted him."

"What!" She whipped her head my way. "Shut the front door. You actually have a date?"

"Look at the road!" I implored loudly.

She focused back on driving. "Sorry, but I can't believe it. When were you going to tell us?"

"I wanted to surprise you in person."

"Give me all the details," she demanded.

"Well, he's a proctologist." I waited for the laughter. And did it ever come.

Tara started uncontrollably giggling. She started snorting for how hard she was laughing.

"It's a very respectable career. He really helped Stu out with his hemorrhoid issue."

She kept chuckling while taking our exit at a frightening

speed, only to blow through a very yellow light. If we survived, it was going to be a miracle. "And you're okay knowing a man who specializes in rectal issues might touch you?"

When she put it that way, it didn't sound all that appealing. But... "Stu says he's meticulous about washing his hands when he walks into the exam room." Hygiene was a must on the list I had given to Hal and Stu.

"I would be, too, if I touched butts all day long." She grinned over at me.

"Oh, ha ha." I grabbed my phone from my bag and pulled up the picture of Dr. Seth Kristoff I'd found on his clinic's website. We would see if she thought it was still funny after she saw how attractive the thirty-six-year-old doctor, who had never been married and believed in being punctual, was. Stu had assured me he had done a thorough interview of Seth while he was helping him with his little "problem." Stu said Dr. Kristoff met all my qualifications and then some.

"At the next stoplight, if you don't run it, I'll show you a picture of him."

"I'm not running them. I'm casually pausing."

I rolled my eyes.

"Thanks to me, we are totally going to be on time."

"If we live," I deadpanned.

"Don't you worry—we will all live to see you walk down the aisle this fall."

I rubbed my lips together. "That sounds so close."

"Hey, Jolene's mom only knew her last two husbands for a few days before she married them."

Pauline. She was a character. But she was no role model. Don't get me wrong: we all loved her. Including Jolene, who had a very unusual childhood. She used a lot of her experiences in her comedy bit about growing up with a woman who took her wherever the wind blew. One of Jolene's funniest routines began with, "What native Tennessee mother names their daughter Jolene? Was she predicting my future, or did she just hate me?"

It referred to Dolly Parton's wildly popular song "Jolene," about a man-stealing woman. Another one of Jolene's zingers began with making fun of the fact that she was conceived in Cancún during spring break and all her mom could tell her about her father was he was from North or South Dakota and every single one of his tattoos was spelled wrong. Jolene would say something like, "With a start to life like that, I was bound to end up in the prison system."

I would say this about Pauline: for as carefree as she was, she always put Jolene first and made sure her daughter had every opportunity. Unlike my parents, who only thought of themselves.

"That's so not comforting," I replied.

Tara halted, screeching her tires, at the next red light she had most likely pondered running. "So maybe Pauline isn't the best example. Show me the doctor."

I held up my phone, displaying a photo of a very handsome man with eyes as blue as the sea and a strong jawline like Henry Cavill's.

"Ooh la la. He's gorgeous enough to make me forget he's shoving his hands up anuses all day long."

That made me snort laugh.

As soon as the light turned green, she went all fast and furious. "When is your date?"

I held on to the door handle for dear life. "Wednesday. I'm meeting him at a cozy French café in Greenville."

"I'm sure you've already checked out the menu and know what you'll be ordering."

"Of course." I made no attempt to hide my weirdness. She was well aware.

She reached over and patted my knee. I was wearing a cute overall dress with tights and booties. It was much more subdued than the sleeveless sequined jumpsuit Tara was rocking. My friends were fashion risk-takers, and I was not. Jolene was sure to be in something leather or leopard print or a combination of the two. No doubt she'd be rocking stilettos while she was at it. The girl was six feet tall and owned every inch. She towered over me and Tara, who were both around five foot six. With that said, you can't wear sequins or leopard print and stay invisible. Hence my boring outfit.

"I'm excited for you." She gave my knee a little squeeze.

"I'm excited for me, too. It's been a while." I looked out the window. It was all familiar, yet it felt so foreign. Sometimes it seemed that my time in Tennessee was a lifetime ago, or more like someone else's life. I'd come to live in Nashville when I was nineteen to go to school after attending a community college in South Carolina. I'd ended up getting a full-ride scholarship to the university here after winning a writing contest. Nana encouraged me to go even though it meant working two jobs just to pay for rent and food. But it was worth it. Not only did I meet Jolene and Tara, who were both student journalists while I served as the editor for the school's newspaper, but I learned I could do hard things. Like helping Tara and Jolene pass all their classes. They loved the study charts and pretests I would make for them every time final exams rolled around. And sometimes I learned I could even step outside my comfort zone when I had to. But that was exhausting.

I think that was a good word for Josh's life—exhausting. Not that he exhausted me. He didn't. No, he enlivened me in ways I didn't know were possible. But his life and this town were too much for me. All the glaring lights and perpetually packed streets full of concert and clubgoers were not my cup of tea. My cup of tea was being curled up with a good book and sipping tea. Throw a man in there, too. There was nothing I loved more than being at home with Josh on a rainy day when we had nowhere to be, snuggled up together, looking up fascinating facts. But Josh wasn't meant to be only mine. The world was his stage, and I refused to be selfish.

There had to be someone else out there for me who didn't have the world constantly begging for his attention. Maybe I could be enough for that man, even with my quirkiness. As a bonus, I would bring Alec into the relationship.

Tara found a parking spot in a paid lot not too far away. My stomach dropped looking at all the people wrapped around the building waiting to get into the club. I was happy so many people were clamoring to see my friend. I just wished visiting this club didn't mean having to see Josh's head painted on the side of the building in the company of some other famous comedians who had performed there as well. Even with a brick canvas as the background, he was cute. He had this Paul Rudd, boy-next-door vibe about him. Attractive, but not overly so. It was more his personality that made you fall in love with him.

Tara grabbed my hand. "I know this is a big deal for you, but you got this. Forget about what's-his-name, even though his pictures are plastered all over the walls." She cringed. "Just don't look at anything inside."

I nodded, feeling like I might vomit if I spoke. I needed to tune into my inner Alec, focusing on gratitude and envisioning the night as I wished it to go. I saw myself bravely walking in and sitting at a table near the stage so I could cheer on my best friend. Of course, I was going to be laughing hysterically—mostly on the inside, because I would be too self-conscious to laugh too loudly. But Jolene would know by my smile and shaking shoulders that I was all in for her performance. I also envisioned, or more like fervently prayed, no one would recognize me.

It's not like Josh ever posted about us. We shared the need for privacy in that way. Although he had seemed to change his tune during his engagement to Camila. They'd plastered selfies of themselves everywhere. Josh had even done the same kind of over-the-top proposal he previously deemed comedic. Whatever. He was my past, and what he did with his life was his own business; you know, except every week when I stalked him for twenty minutes like I had today at the airport while I was waiting for my late flight. I should probably stop doing that. Today would be my last stalking episode, I vowed. I would close my alt account and unfollow him everywhere. I didn't need to know that he was house hunting in LA and making funny videos to mock the process or that he still had a defined chest.

"Let's go," I said before I lost my nerve. I opened my door when Tara got a text.

"Just a sec." She pulled out her phone and went ashen.

"Everything okay?"

"Uh . . . yeah . . . yeah. Jolene just wanted to make sure we got here. She says it's best for us not to meet her in the greenroom. It's a zoo," she stammered.

"Is she okay?"

"Oh, yeah," Tara said in pitch well above her normal soprano voice.

"Are you sure?"

"Absolutely," she laughed maniacally.

"You're scaring me."

She took a deep breath in and let it out slowly. "I'm fine. Everything is A-okay." She sounded like she said that more to herself than to me.

"If you say so."

"I do." She grabbed her silk coat and flew out of the car.

I grabbed my jacket and met her outside in the just-at-freezing temps, the frigid humidity hitting me in the face. "Do we need to get in line, then?" I wasn't looking forward to waiting out in the cold, though they should be opening the doors soon.

"She said to go to the front; Mikey will let us cut in line."

"Mikey, as in the owner?" My stomach rolled in nauseous waves.

"Hey, Mikey loves you. He always asks how you're doing. He's going to be so happy to see you again."

I did like Mikey. He was always good to me, making sure there were fresh fruits and veggies in the greenroom for me whenever Josh was performing.

Tara came around the car, sparkling in the light of the streetlamps, and grabbed my hand. "Come on."

I followed her like a zombie, except much faster. She was on a mission, halting traffic in the middle of the street so we could cross. I didn't know what the big hurry was since we weren't meeting Jolene before the show. It bummed me out I couldn't wish her luck in person. I wondered why the greenroom was crazy. It was normally just for the opening and major acts and whomever their guests were. Tara and I were Jolene's people, and I couldn't imagine Kegan Carr, the opening act, had an entourage. From his social media accounts I gathered this was probably the biggest gig he had done.

Tara meant business, marching us past the crowd of people blowing into their hands and huddling together for warmth. We got a lot of stares asking who we thought we were to cut to the front of the line.

We almost made it to the entrance when Mikey called out, waving his arm, "Tara, Natalie, this way!"

I swallowed my heart down and reentered the world I had been so thrilled to leave behind.

five

"Natalie. It's been too long. It's so good to see you." Mikey wrapped me up in a bear hug as soon as we made it into the lobby. He was a big, burly man who looked more like a lumberjack than a club owner. He was even wearing a flannel shirt. His fuzzy salt-and-pepper beard tickled my cheek.

"How are you?" I asked, muffled against his chest, breathing in his Old Spice scent.

"Business is booming. I can't ask for more than that." He let go of me and it was like a switch flipped. All the pleasantries were over. "We better get you to your seats. Hurry."

I looked at Tara in a *What's his deal?* sort of way. Maybe he really hated me. He was probably just pretending a moment ago for Tara and Jolene's sake.

Tara acted just as weird and grabbed my hand. "Let's do this."

What was all the rushing about? "What's going on?" I said for Tara's ears only.

She didn't have time to answer.

"Sorry, ladies, I can't put you up front tonight," Mikey lamented while veering us to the left of the stage toward a table that wasn't too far back, but it wasn't at the best angle. For the first time in my life, I wanted to be front and center to show

Jolene how much I loved and supported her. I expected Tara to get all southern belle on him and make a big fuss, but she said not a word.

My heart started pounding to the beat of "We Will Rock You," which meant only one thing. I was going to have to step far outside my comfort zone. I seriously hated when that happened. "Uh, Mikey," I breathed. "Is there any way we could sit closer? Maybe even share a table with another party? This is a big night for Jolene, and we want to do our best to support her."

Mikey paused and rubbed his meaty neck, giving me an uncomfortable smile. "Aw, kid . . . the truth is—"

"The truth is that Jolene is super anxious, and she thinks it's best if she can't directly see us," Tara butted in.

I blinked a few times, not sure I'd heard her right. That didn't sound like Jolene at all. Jolene was normally like a racehorse, begging to get out of the gate, full of excitement and a conquering attitude. She had nerves of steel.

Mikey cleared his throat. "Yeah, yeah, what she said."

"Maybe we should go back and reassure her," I suggested, more worried than ever about my friend.

"No!" Tara screeched.

"Are you okay?" I had to ask. She was acting very odd.

Her shoulders rose and fell dramatically. "I'm fine. It's just Jolene really doesn't want us back there. She's uh . . . meditating."

My brow quirked. "Really?" I'd been trying to get her to do it for years with me, but she called it kooky.

"Yep. She finally gave it a try, and who'd have known? She loves it." Tara tittered nervously.

I eyed my best friend carefully. Something was rotten in the state of Denmark. That I knew. I just didn't know what.

"Please have a seat," Mikey directed us. "Order anything. It's on the house tonight." He kissed my cheek. "It really is good to see you, kid. Don't leave without saying goodbye. Good luck." He dashed off.

"Good luck?" I questioned.

"Well . . . I'm sure he knows how hard it is for you to be back here."

He had no idea. Now that my little burst of bravery was wearing off, a tidal wave of emotions and memories were coming at me like a tsunami. I couldn't help but think of all the time I spent here with Josh. I remembered waiting in the greenroom with him on his favorite chair, an old plaid one that had seen better days. He would pull me onto his lap and whisper things that would make me blush and giggle. He called it his warm-up routine. Once he told me the sound of my lyrical laughter felt like Christmas morning to him. Each time he heard it, it filled him with the same excitement he had as a child running down the stairs to see what Santa had brought him. Then I would stand in the wings and watch him. At the beginning of every show, before he ever said a word, he would look my way and wink. He said that was his way of saying, "I love you." I would mouth those words back, and seconds later, he magically owned the crowd—owned my heart.

Tara grabbed my arm and forcefully sat me in the chair with the worst view of the stage.

"She doesn't want to see me at all?"

"Of course she does. I just thought you would appreciate being a bit out of the way. You know, just in case anyone you know is here tonight." Her eyes darted all over the place as other patrons started piling in.

"Did you see someone?" I hated to ask, feeling as if someone had turned the heat way up. I shrugged out of my jacket.

"Not yet . . . I mean no." She sat down and fanned herself.

"You're so red. Do you want to go to the ladies' room and splash some water on your cheeks?"

"Uh, no. Do you know how long it took me to get the contouring right? Besides, we don't want anyone to steal our seats."

That was a good idea. I pulled my phone out and kept my

head down in case anyone I knew came in and recognized me. "I'm not being rude," I said out of the side of my mouth. "I'm just trying to be invisible."

"Good idea," Tara said, to my surprise.

My head popped up.

Tara flashed me an innocent smile. "I just want you to feel comfortable. Keep that gorgeous head of yours as far down as you would like. Heck, pull up a book on your phone. You do you."

I looked around at the great swelling of people clamoring to get a table or a seat. I started feeling itchy. "Are you sure you don't mind? I'm all on board when Jolene hits the stage."

"Not. At. All. We're just proud you rearranged your schedule and showed up."

I was pretty proud of that, too. So proud, I put a figurative star on my chart. I was supposed to be starting a new book for a client today, and I had to move up my wax, polish, and shine day. But I'd made it work, even if it gave me heartburn. Admittedly, it was a little freeing to live on the wild side. Or you know, wild for me.

"Thanks for being my emotional support extrovert." I pulled up the latest book I was reading on my phone. I was reliving my childhood. Nana would read to me from the Noel Streatfeild books she had borrowed from the library. I was currently rereading *Skating Shoes*. Those books made me know I wanted to do something in the literary arts. Editing was a natural fit for me. Believe me, I was meticulous.

"Anytime." Tara started tapping her leg. I assumed she was nervous for Jolene, but I had no doubt our best friend would pull off tonight in a grand fashion.

The minutes ticked away as I read about Harriet Johnson and her family. Thankfully, not one person from the past had shown up, at least not that I could see. I was sure there were some, as Jolene and Josh had mutual friends and acquaintances. As long as they stayed away from me, I would survive. Hopefully.

Love Rescheduled

The blaring country music faded, as did the house lights. The spotlight hit the stage as Mikey came out to play emcee. He loved that part of the job.

"Welcome to Laugh on Tap!" he shouted into the mic, and the crowd cheered. "We have an amazing show in store for you tonight. First things first, though: in honor of our headliner, Miss Jolene, it's ladies' night, so every drink on tap is half off for the fairer sex."

Tara and I cheered when he mentioned Jolene's name. By *cheered*, I mean Tara screamed her name, and I clapped, yelling her name in my head.

Mikey went over a few house rules, including no recording or flash photography, before getting ready to introduce the opening act. "Like I said, tonight is going to be amazing. We have a surprise guest all the way from LA."

Tara slinked down in her chair.

Meanwhile, I perked right up—or rather, felt like I might have a heart attack—when I heard "LA." Surely he did not mean—

"That's right, ladies and gents, our hometown boy has returned. Give it up for Josh Keller!" He put the mic back into the stand.

My worst nightmare came to life as I sat frozen. I didn't know what to do. I wasn't sure I could do anything, as I felt paralyzed.

Tara reached across the table for me.

I remained motionless.

"I'm so sorry," she mouthed.

That breathed a bit of life back into me. "Did you know?" I cried, trying to keep my voice down, though the crowd's uproar was deafening. Everyone was on their feet, except for Tara and me.

"I swear we didn't know until tonight. He showed up unexpectedly."

All the hurrying and table situation made sense now. Why

didn't Tara just tell me? I could have just left. Of course, that's why she didn't tell me. She wanted me to stay to support Jolene. Which I absolutely wanted to do, but I couldn't see Josh. I was never even supposed to be in the same zip code as him. "What do I do?" I begged to know.

It was too late to do anything. Josh ran out on the stage in his signature fit-me-to-a-T jeans and Rod Stewart shirt. Josh showed his affinity for seventies artists and rock bands by wearing a concert tee anytime he was onstage. Of course, I was his polar opposite and loved jazz and classical music. Tragically, Josh was just as cute as ever with his boyish charm. Dang him.

I grabbed a menu and held it in front of my face while slouching in my seat. Thoughts of army crawling across the club to the exit filled my head to the point I had moved beyond envisioning it to the actual planning phase. Alec's training was coming in handy. Except I could hear him say, *"Off the record, this is a terrible idea."*

"He's still doing the ridiculous dance moves when he comes on the stage," Tara commented.

I had to press my lips together. I could picture every cheesy move as the crowd went even more wild. He used to practice them in the bathroom mirror as he got ready. How many times had I heard him sing "Da Ya Think I'm Sexy?" by the man on his T-shirt? It was part of his daily routine.

"Don't let him see you," I implored.

"He knows Jolene is here."

My heart pounded harder. "Does he know I'm here?"

"Not yet."

That didn't make me feel better. I had to escape.

"What's up, Nashville?" Josh said in his I'm-so-cool voice. "It's good to be back home. Where are my Nashville homies?"

Several people in the audience cheered. One woman shouted over the crowd, "I love you, Josh!"

"Hey, hey, girl, slow down. There's plenty of time for that tonight."

The crowd laughed.

"But honestly, it's great to be back in Nashville. Everything is better here than in LA. The food, the music, the women," he said sexily.

I could hear all the women swooning. I rolled my eyes and shimmied down farther in my seat until my head was practically level with the table. The only thing I cared about was hiding from Josh, even though I looked like an idiot.

"Speaking of women, I used to date a girl who had to schedule everything..."

Oh. My. Gosh. Surely he wasn't talking about me. He'd promised me he would never, ever use me in any of his jokes. We are talking about a fairy tale promise with dire consequences. Just the thought of him possibly using me as material had me dropping the menu.

"And I mean *everything*..."

Tara whipped her head toward me, knowing there was no doubt who Josh was talking about. I did schedule *everything*. It took away all the anxiety of it. That wasn't to say I didn't welcome spontaneous affection. I did—it's just ... well ... it didn't matter.

In a gut reaction, I sat up, so much blood rushing to my head. I could hardly make out what he was saying, but it was definitely about intimate things. Things he had no business talking about.

The crowd was going nuts over it.

His casualness about it and the audience's laughter incensed me to the point that all I cared about was leaving, not paying heed to the consequences of getting out of my seat. So, I popped up like a jack-in-the-box even as Tara was reaching for me.

Almost as if Josh had a radar detection system that was homed in on me, he looked my way at exactly the wrong moment. Our eyes locked. He stopped mid-sentence and dropped the mic, sending an earsplitting noise throughout the club. "Nat?" he said like he was out of breath.

I didn't have to look around to know every head in the club was ping-ponging between us. Every introvert cell in my body was crying, begging for us to get out of there. So that's what I did. I turned and fled like my life depended on it, weaving in and out of tables, trying not to trip on anyone's bag or chair.

"Stop that woman!" Josh called out. "Her. The gorgeous redhead." I imagined him pointing at me, but I didn't dare turn around.

What the what? Was he freaking insane? The crowd looked as bewildered as I felt. Maybe they thought this was part of his act. I wasn't sure, but no one made a move to stop me, so I kept on going. I almost made it to the bar when Josh yelled out, "Stop her! She's a thief."

My head about exploded when I spun in my high-heeled booties and glared at the stupid, stupid man. Why would he say something so grossly untrue? I felt like I was back in the junior high talent show, wishing to be saved, knowing no Hugh Grant was on the horizon. Every insecurity I ever felt began swimming through my head.

The crowd remained stunned and in their seats. But Josh's lie ignited a fire with the security team. Two big bouncer-like creatures came at me like they were relatives of Tweedledee and Tweedledum.

Josh flashed me his signature *I'm so charming, you know you love me* grin.

But I definitely did not love him at the moment. In fact, I loathed him.

When the Tweedle brothers approached me, I spluttered, "I didn't steal anything."

They looked at the stage and Josh for direction. Tweedledum said, "She says she didn't steal anything."

Mortified didn't even begin to cover it. I was going to have to have a session with Alec every day for a month to work through this. The bill was going to Josh.

I glared harder at Josh, daring him to contradict me.

Tara came to join me. She, too, was throwing Josh dirty looks.

"She's lying," Josh said, as serious as could be.

"You pr—" Tara started to call him her favorite word, *prick*, when Mikey jumped into the fray. "Hey, folks, I think there's been a big misunderstanding here. Natalie and Tara, why don't you come with me?"

Whispers in the crowd began. "Natalie? As in his ex-girlfriend?"

I was beyond loathing Josh now. I abhorred him, which was the strongest way to express hate in the English language, according to my thesaurus, which I always kept handy.

Mikey gently took my arm. "Come on, honey. Let's go backstage."

I blindly let him guide me. I couldn't breathe and was sure to pass out at any moment. I'd rather it not be in front of a crowd—or Josh's watchful eye. The traitor. If I didn't have an aneurysm, I was so getting over him. He wouldn't be hindering any future relationships of mine. That was if I could bring myself to have one. I might have to go into hiding after this. If I wasn't mistaken, some flashes had gone off in the crowd. If this didn't make the rounds on social media, it would be a miracle.

I wasn't sure how we got backstage, but Jolene was to me in seconds, throwing her arms around me. "Nat, I'm so sorry. I didn't know he was going to be here tonight. I swear." She let go of me.

"It's my fault," Mikey chimed in. "He called me this morning to see if he could stop by. How could I refuse? He's made this place what it is today. And I knew you were coming, but I thought, hell, maybe it would be good for you to see each other again."

He was dead wrong, but I was too numb to say anything. All my planning and careful life construction could never have prepared me for this. I was going to need to schedule a breakdown in the very near future.

Six

"I THINK SHE'S GONE CATATONIC," Tara worried, waving her hand in front of my face.

I blinked and blinked, wishing I could blink out of existence. How could this have happened to me? I was a nice enough girl who baked holiday treats for neighbors, and every Sunday I took dinner to Hal and Stu. All I wanted out of life was to live in my cozy little cocoon of comfort and safety. Was that too much to ask for? I'd had my fill of awful and humiliating situations. Josh, more than anyone, knew that. Only he knew that once when my mother was drunk, she'd told me she wished she never had me. Or that I always spelled the first word wrong on purpose in any spelling bee they forced me to do in elementary school, even though I knew every word, just so I didn't have to be in front of anyone. And I had only ever shared the talent show incident with him.

So, for him to create more humiliation in my life hurt all the more.

Josh obviously didn't care. In the background, the crowd was laughing hysterically at his jokes, which I still wasn't comprehending. I was doing my best to tune him out. I longed to leave, but I looked at Tara and Jolene, who stared at me, deep concern etched into their features. They were my people, my rocks. I asked myself what they would do in my situation. Besides maiming Josh, they would do the hard thing and stay and support me. I knew that's what I had to do. I would stay and cheer on my best friend. All from the safety of backstage. I wasn't stepping one foot out into the main area until every person was gone, including the waitstaff.

Jolene placed her hands on my shoulders and gave me a little shake. "Come on, Nat. Snap out of it. You got this. At least breathe."

On her cue, I took in a big gulp of air and let it out.

"There you go." Jolene grinned. She looked stunning. Her amazing dark curls framed her beautiful face. Her aqua eyes were screaming that this was her night. That made me come to my senses. I didn't want anything else to detract from her big moment.

"I'm fine," I lied for a good cause.

"No, you're not, but good try." Jolene gave me a squeeze. She was right—I was so not all right.

To make matters worse, Zac, Josh's best friend, entered the picture. He was in the wings, closer to the stage. I wasn't surprised to see him. He and Josh had been best friends since high school. They got into all sorts of mischief together. Zac was still Josh's right-hand man. He filmed and edited all of Josh's videos. He even appeared in several of them and frequently talked off camera, asking Josh questions or giving fake advice.

As he walked toward me, sneering, I could mentally hear "Toccata in D Minor" going off in my head. It went well with the horror film I was currently starring in.

Zac was on the shorter side and overly buff, in my opinion. The guy was constantly lifting weights. His spiky golden hair was reminiscent of a caricature, which was fitting, since he was about as mature as most cartoon characters. There was no love lost between us. We got along well enough for Josh's benefit, but I always felt like Zac was using Josh—riding his coattails, even.

Zac was shaking his head, his beady eyes focused on me. "What are you doing here?"

"Watch yourself," Tara warned him.

Zac didn't intimidate me. I knew he never liked me. He was always team Camila. Zac thought I was a bore. He wasn't wrong. Boring was safe. Look what happened to me trying to get out of my comfort zone tonight.

"I'm here to support my best friend, much like you," I threw back at him.

He shrugged as if it wasn't a good enough explanation for him.

I didn't care what he thought.

"Stay away from Josh. You really messed with his head," he spewed. "And the last thing he needs right now is for you to screw up what could be the biggest deal of his career."

What did he mean, I messed with his head? I never toyed with Josh. And why would he think I would screw up whatever deal he was talking about? I only ever wanted the best for Josh. It's why I had walked away. Besides, I had no power over him. We hadn't even seen each other in three years. I didn't get to question Zac, as Josh was taking his bow from the sound of it. It was time for me to focus on Jolene and forget I would more than likely come face-to-face with my ex, whom I abhorred.

I plastered on the fakest of smiles for Jolene. "You're going to kill it."

"I want to kill something." Jolene narrowed her eyes at Zac.

Zac went ashen, obviously intimidated. Did that bring me some pleasure? Oh, yes.

"Let's play nice," Mikey jumped in. "You can kill him after the show." He didn't sound like he was teasing. I guess I wasn't the only one who didn't have any love for Zac.

Zac took that as his cue to head to the greenroom.

Jolene stood taller, filled with a sense of pride for intimidating the weasel.

Tara pulled me into a group hug with Jolene. "You got this. We will be here watching the entire time."

"Absolutely," I agreed, though I was shaking in my booties, literally and figuratively. Any moment now, Josh was going to come off that stage. I prayed he would keep on walking, although part of me wanted to confront him and shame him for what he had done to me minutes ago.

"Thank you." Jolene fiercely hugged us.

Mikey headed for the stage, but not before giving me a look of condolence as he walked by.

Jolene let go of us and closed her eyes, getting ready for her big moment.

Tara and I stood by, holding hands. I begged myself to not make this about me and stay focused on Jolene. Josh was ancient history. Jolene and Tara would always be my present and future.

In what seemed like a dream montage, Josh appeared in front of me, just as Mikey was introducing Jolene.

I stopped breathing as Josh planted himself across from Tara and me near some mic stands. His rich chocolate eyes lasered in on me as if willing me to stay in place. He didn't need to worry; he had sufficiently paralyzed me.

"I never thought I would say this to you, but you're a prick," Tara lobbed his way, seemingly happy she finally got to say her piece. Her grip on my hand tightened.

Josh didn't even flinch. His eyes stayed right on me.

I said nothing, desperately trying to keep my eye on the prize, Jolene. Yet Josh was making it difficult. So many emotions swirled inside me while staring at the infuriating man. While I more than loathed him, there was no denying I still loved him. I ached to touch the curls of hair that played around his ears when he let his hair grow out like it was now. I longed to see his smile, which made his dimples appear. Mostly, I wished for him to tell me he didn't hate me. Hypocritical, considering I felt all sorts of hate for him.

Zac came back with a towel for Josh, who had sweat

dripping down his face because of the stage lights. That used to be my job. "Come on, man, let's get out of here." He scowled at me, warning me not to engage with Josh.

Josh ignored him. It was clear he wasn't moving an inch.

"Oh, hell," Zac muttered before throwing the towel at him and stomping off like a petulant child.

Josh easily caught the thing, yet he remained steady, making sure I didn't move.

Tara looked between the two of us. "Well, I guess this is going to be awkward."

Awkward didn't even cover it. What was Josh's deal? Why wouldn't he leave?

I tore my gaze away from him, remembering tonight wasn't about me. As soon as Mikey said, "Please welcome to the stage Jolene Carmichael," Tara and I hooted and hollered the best we could. I even mustered up a real yell. Did I regret it instantly? Yes. But it wasn't about me.

Jolene started, and for a second, I could pretend like Josh wasn't unnaturally gaping at me.

"Thank you, thank you," Jolene began. "You know, this place reminds me of my mom's house. Brick walls, smells like cheap perfume, lots of strangers coming in and out laughing at me."

That got the crowd going.

"Good one," I mouthed to Tara.

Jolene went on with her shtick about being named Jolene and crazy stories about her mom that sounded fake but were all true. Then she did her new bit about the joys of where she had found glitter on her person. It was hilarious. The audience was eating it up. Jolene shined the entire time.

Meanwhile, Josh never moved a muscle. I would admit to glancing at him a few times. Apparently, he was determined we speak to one another. Oh, did I have some things to say to him after he'd mortified me and lied about me in front of hundreds of people. I was a lot of things, but a thief wasn't one of them.

Love Rescheduled

When Jolene made her final bow for the night, Tara and I shouted another round of cheers. I was so proud to call her my friend. She absolutely killed it. But I had a feeling I was about to die inside. There was no way Josh was going to let me leave without some sort of confrontation. It wouldn't be a shocking revelation to learn that confrontations weren't my strong suit. Josh loved to face things head-on. He used to love to make me do the same, especially in our relationship. If something he did or a situation bothered me, he wanted to know about it. Not to say he always agreed with my assessments. Oh, no. Josh was a world-class arguer. He really should have been a lawyer. I had to admit; he was good at owning up and apologizing when he did things wrong. Sometimes, I swore he egged on an argument just so we could make up. And could he ever make up.

I needed to stop thinking about the making up; it had me feeling weak in the knees, wishing to do just that. That wasn't going to be helpful to anyone. I wondered if Josh ever regretted making me feel so comfortable around him that I could easily tell him off. My parents had never even afforded me the luxury of having my own opinion growing up. Sadly, I hadn't even known couples could have civilized arguments and then forgive each other and be stronger for it. For a long time, I didn't even know I could be right. Josh had taught me that.

Still, confrontation made me feel queasy. It all went back to the ego thing. Whose voice did I hear? Unfortunately, I heard my parents' voices all too often telling me all the things I did wrong. That I wasn't enough. Part of me now felt like I deserved Josh's earlier humiliation, as messed up as that sounded. Intellectually, I knew that was wrong, but it was hard to shake.

Jolene floated off the stage, smiling from ear to ear.

I was so happy for her. She deserved every second of her triumph. I tried my best to convey how proud I was as I embraced her once she finally made it our way. Words seemed inadequate. Funny, as I considered myself something of a wordsmith. But I knew sometimes a touch said a hundred times more than anything mere words could.

Jolene held on to me as if she knew she was protecting me from what I would face as soon as we let go. "You can do this," she whispered in my ear. "Who knows, maybe this is just what you need," she said mysteriously.

I leaned away from her, resisting the urge to disagree with her on her big night. Truly, I wanted this to be all about her. I should have just stayed in my seat and behind the menu until Josh exited the stage. I wasn't good in unexpected situations. Hence my need for schedules. Like I said, I was going to put Alec on speed dial for the next month.

Tara and I weren't the only ones wanting to congratulate Jolene. It meant I had to leave the safety of her arms. In a coward's move, I turned and rushed past Josh, pretending as if he hadn't just stood there for forty-five minutes staring at me. Where I was going, I didn't know. And it didn't matter.

Josh had other ideas. He gently grabbed my arm. Even through my blouse, his touch sent a shiver down my body that I could feel in my toes. His touch was like a welcome home, but I knew it was to a house that was too big and scary for me, like a haunted house but with great lighting and designer furniture.

"We need to talk," he said lowly.

Did we really, though? I thought that going the passive-aggressive route might be more appropriate. That meant unfollowing him with my alt account. That would really show him. Instead, I found myself following him to the only dressing room on the premises. I desperately tried not to think of the steamy things that had ensued in said room. All unscheduled affection, thank you very much.

Josh opened the door with a large gold star on it and waved me in.

I tiptoed past him, and his Obsession for Men scent hit me. The corners of my lips twitched, thinking of all the times I'd teased him for wearing the popular eighties cologne he claimed was his signature scent. So maybe it still turned me on.

"Do you find me amusing?" There was a hint of hope in his voice.

"Not at all." Ire for what he had done tonight flowed in my veins, begging to be unleashed.

When he shut the door, leaned against it, and began perusing me, the ire was almost to its boiling point. I hadn't argued with anyone in almost three years. Weird, I kind of missed it, as much as I didn't enjoy it. Maybe it was because it meant there was something worth fighting for in my life. I had tried to fight for my relationship with Josh. It just got too hard. All I wanted for him was to live his dreams and be happy. I knew he couldn't do that with me.

"I can't believe you're here." A hint of affection lingered in his voice, which honestly irked me after what he had done on the stage tonight.

The boiling point hit with fervor. "I can't believe you accused me in front of everyone of being a thief. What's wrong with you? I've never stolen a thing."

He folded his arms, smugly. "That's not true."

"What have I stolen?"

His faced pinched, making him look menacing. It was a look I had never seen on him. His eyes bored straight into mine. "You stole *everything*. You stole us."

That knocked the air right out of me, making me fall back and sink into the couch. The couch that had seen a lot of action. I couldn't think of that right now, or ever. I had more pressing matters at hand. Like how I had hurt my ex. The pain was apparent in his eyes. Yet . . . "You moved on awfully quickly."

"Don't bring Camila into this."

"Right," I scoffed. His precious Camila.

"I know what you're thinking. And you're wrong."

"Am I?" I practically begged him to tell me I was mistaken. That he was faithful to me.

"Dead wrong. You have no idea—" he stopped himself short.

"You're right. I had no idea what a liar you were," I said as waspishly as possible.

"You promised me you would never use me in your routine."

He stepped closer. "Yeah, well, you promised you would always love me, so I guess we're both liars."

"Who says I haven't kept my promise?" I gasped and covered my mouth.

His face fell slack.

Oh, how I wish I hadn't said that. He had no business knowing I was still in love with him. I jumped up and lunged for the door. I needed to talk to Alec ASAP.

"Nat, stop. Please," he pleaded.

I paused, almost as if in midair.

"I'm sorry. I shouldn't have told that joke. If it makes you feel better, it was always the best hour of my day. Of my life," he added quietly.

Oh, mine too. "Goodbye, Josh," my voice cracked. I hoped it was the last time I had to say those words. I wasn't sure I could ever utter them again.

Seven

"How are you?" Jolene and Tara asked in unison over the phone. Their voices echoed on speaker in the one and only bathroom in my small cottage. It was early Monday morning, and I was doing my getting-ready routine. I was running a flat iron through a few pieces of my pixie cut to give direction and a bit of volume to it before I went in with the styling wax. Jolene and Tara had convinced me to go with the bold cut right after we'd graduated from college. They said it went perfectly with my heart-shaped face and to-die-for cheekbones. Their bias was obvious, but I appreciated it all the same. More than that, I was thankful they made me go outside my comfort zone every once in a while, the past few days not included. No surprise, I used to hide my face behind my long hair. With this cut, there was no hiding at all. It kind of felt like my life right now: exposed.

We had made a fairy tale promise over the weekend not to discuss my fiasco with Josh, even though my best friends were dying to do so. But I had sworn to make the weekend about Jolene, and unlike Josh, I'd kept my word. That meant I went to the after-parties both nights, even though people were obviously whispering to their friends about what had happened at the club. Jolene and Tara did their best to shield me, but it was hard to miss all the pointing and gawking. Thank goodness for corners and books.

I was still processing all the events. Especially the moment when Josh told me I had stolen everything from him. How could that be true? He'd gotten engaged to Camila. And believe me, they looked mighty happy about it on social media. At that point, I was still crying every day, mourning our relationship.

So, let's see, how was I? Well, I was still breathing, which was a miracle, seeing as a video of me looking like a deer in the headlights at Laugh on Tap was circulating around social media. If that wasn't enough humiliation, Josh posted about it. I should have unfollowed him sooner. His post was apologetic. Something to the tune of, *I need to apologize for my behavior Friday night. It was unprofessional, and I didn't mean to hurt anyone. Blah, blah, blah.* He didn't use my name, but everyone who had seen the video knew it was me. Which meant they were connecting the dots that I was a liar, or the woman who scheduled intimacy. Either way, it was a lose-lose situation. I was thinking about the witness protection program.

Alec promised me two hours today. I happily rearranged my schedule. That's how desperate I was for his help. It was also why I was talking to my best friends earlier than normal. I needed all the reinforcements I could get.

I looked into the small circular mirror above the pink sink Nana loved, which was why I hadn't replaced it, and stared into my pale-green eyes, which were shining brighter thanks to all the red lines brought on by a lack of sleep. "I'm going to go with not well."

"It will die down soon," Jolene tried to console me. "There's always a new story."

"I'll go all Taylor Swift and drop hints about who I'm actually trashing in my books," Tara offered. "That could take off some heat." She had a huge following online. Her fans were dying to know the real men behind her antagonists, and the protagonists, too.

I set my straightener down and smiled. "I love you, ladies.

Thank you, but you'll sell more books if you keep up the mystery."

They both laughed.

"So, uh, what did you and Josh talk about?" Jolene could hold out no longer.

I gripped the counter. "Not much, other than he said I stole everything from him."

Their gasps filled the bathroom.

"Yeah," I breathed out.

"How does that make you feel?" Tara asked, like she was Dr. Phil.

"Awful, but also confused. He obviously moved on. Besides, he embarrassed me. I'm doing my best to abhor him." I'm not going to lie: our little conversation had added some difficulty to that plan, but at the same time, the video circulating around social media was fueling the hate fire.

"Total douche move," Jolene added.

"I'm writing him into my next book." Tara evilly laughed.

"I can't wait to edit it. I may add some of my own embellishments." That could be therapeutic.

"But you're still going on your date with the proctologist," Tara snorted, "right?"

After letting out a deep breath, I reached for my lip gloss. "I don't know. I'm thinking about going into hiding. Can you contact the US Marshals yourself?"

"You really want to give control of your life over to a government entity? And cut off all contact with us?" Jolene sounded put out.

"Of course not. Fine, witness protection is out. What about moving to a foreign country? I've been using Duolingo to learn French. You could come with me."

"Hmm. Gorgeous French men." Tara contemplated. "Let's think about this one. In the meantime, you need to keep your date. September thirtieth will be here before you know it. And

I've been scouring bridal sites for the perfect bridesmaid's dresses."

"I would hate to deny you the opportunity of a new dress," I teased her. "But how can I go out in public ever again?" I made an exception over the weekend only because I loved Jolene so much.

"Nat," Jolene chimed in. "Josh is big, but he's not a household name. At least not yet. But I've heard rumors about him landing a TV or movie deal."

My heart dropped. Not sure why. It's not like I had any hope Josh and I would get back together. But . . . him being a famous movie or TV star was the final nail in the coffin, so to speak. The last thing I needed in my life was a *more* famous boyfriend. But that was a moot point because I abhorred him. I probably should abhor him a little more, though. The whole "I stole everything from him" was getting to me. I had been anyone's everything. I was going to need to watch that video a lot today and stoke the flames of hate.

"Zac mentioned something about Josh being close to landing the biggest deal of his career, and he didn't want me to screw it up. Like that was even possible. I doubt I'll ever see Josh again." I was banking on it, praying for it, whatever I had to do. Being around him was like a dream and a nightmare rolled into one. I swiped a layer of gloss on my lips to finish getting ready.

"Please send him a wedding announcement." Tara cackled with delight.

I would never do that, especially after the anguish on Josh's face. And he had spared me his announcement with Camila. Or maybe they never even sent them out.

Unexpectedly, my doorbell rang.

"Wow. Amazon is getting earlier all the time." I assumed that's who it was. Who else would come to the door before eight in the morning? Unless Mrs. Pritchard next door needed to borrow an egg or something. It was something Nana and she used to do whenever the occasion arose. I think sometimes she was just lonely. I should make a better effort to check on her.

I took my phone with me so we could continue our conversation for the next few minutes. I had to get off at eight to start work. I would work a couple of hours, take a walking break, and then it was lunch and Alec before I went back to work. It was the beauty of being a freelance editor. This was assuming I could function today. Josh's humiliation and that video were wreaking havoc on my ability to think straight.

"Let me just grab my package." I hoped it was the new dish scrubbers I'd ordered. Was it sad how excited I was about the prospect? Probably.

Without even looking out the tiny windows of the door, I opened it, ready to retrieve my delivery. Instead of dish scrubbers, I got the shock of my life.

"Josh," I spluttered breathlessly, almost dropping my phone.

"What!" I could hear my friends yell.

Josh stood there running a hand through his dark hair, looking as if he hadn't shaved in a few days, or slept, judging by how red and gritty his eyes were. His Rolling Stones T-shirt looked more than wrinkled, like he'd just driven all night.

"What are you doing here?"

Without an invitation, he opened the screen door, which creaked something awful. "We have some unfinished business to take care of."

"And what is that?"

He took a moment to peer into my eyes, owning every part of me. "Us, Nat."

Uh. Say what? I put the phone to my ear. "I'm going to need to call you back," I said in about five different octaves.

All I could hear on the other end was a bunch of yelling and swearing before I hung up.

Josh walked right in like he owned the place. It was then I noticed he had his old duffel bag slung around his shoulder. He'd stuffed the thing with clothes, which were peeking out of the zipper.

"Did you bring your dirty laundry?" It would be just like him to think he could do his laundry while we argued over whatever he considered to be unfinished business. But why would he bring his laundry all this way? Where had he even come from?

He let the duffel bag drop, a smirk on his face. "I'm staying here."

I spat out a maniacal laugh. Was he pranking me? "No, you're not."

"That's not very hospitable of you. What would Nana think of your manners?" That was a low blow bringing my beloved grandmother, who adored the stupid man, into it.

"It's neither here nor there. I didn't invite you."

"Like I said, we have some unfinished business. And I've been driving since two this morning and I'm tired as hell, so where can I crash?"

I blinked at least a hundred times with the widest eyes possible. His audacity was astounding. Add in that it floored me he had driven all night to come here. That was something he would have done when we were a couple. Not now when . . . "Are you insane? You mortified me over the weekend. Now you think you can just show up here and invite yourself to stay with me? I abhor you."

"Going with the next level of hate, are we? Well, here's a news flash for you: I haven't exactly had warm and fuzzy feelings for you the last few years. And to answer your question, I am insane. Having the woman you love walk out on you for no damn reason will do that to a guy."

I faltered a bit, his admission catching me off guard. "You know I had my reasons," I threw back at him. Good ones too.

"Yeah." He scrubbed a hand over his stubbled cheeks. "Your reasons." He let out a heavy breath. "I'm too tired to get into this with you right now." He kicked off his sneakers and walked over to my pristine white couch and threw himself onto it, grabbing a throw pillow and stretching out his tall, lanky body as far as he could. "I'll crash here for now. We can discuss future sleeping arrangements when I wake up." He flashed me a seductive smile.

If he thought that sexy grin of his was getting him anywhere besides the nearest hotel, he had another thing coming. Not to say my heart didn't skip a few beats.

He closed his dreamy chocolate eyes. "Good night, Nat. I'm sorry for embarrassing you."

I stood stunned, gaping at him, not able to form any words. I should have kicked his cute tight butt out of there, but I was confused by how I could hate and love someone so much at the same time. All I knew was, when he woke up, he had to go.

It already devastated me.

Eight

"Well, obviously he has to go," I whispered into the phone to my best friends, who were salivating for an update. Not sure why I was keeping my voice down. Josh slept like the dead. A train could steamroll through the house and he would slumber right through it. I shouldn't even be acting like a good hostess. That didn't stop me from covering him with one of Nana's old quilts she had hand stitched. What I should have done was smothered his face with it. His mere unexpected presence was just a reminder that we were completely incompatible. He was already screwing up my schedule. It's kind of hard to keep your mind on work when your ex shows up unexpectedly and declares you made him go insane and hints that you're still the woman he loves. But loving each other was never our problem.

The incident over the weekend was just proof of what a nightmare Josh's life would be for me. And now that he was about to sign a rumored TV or movie deal, it would only get worse. Like *A Nightmare on Elm Street* level of horror.

Besides, I abhorred him, and I had a date in two days with a doctor who looked like Henry Cavill.

"I have to say, it's kind of romantic," Tara sighed.

"I thought we all agreed we hated him now."

"We do," Tara responded. "But, you have to admit, it's pretty hot. Can I use it in a book?"

"Sure." I rolled my eyes. "I can't believe he's here."

"So, when are you going to tell him you're getting married?" Jolene sounded eager at the prospect. "That should have him running for the hills."

"But I'm not really getting married."

"Not yet," Tara sang.

I thought about it for a moment. I didn't love the idea of divulging my plan to Josh. Not like he didn't already know about all my idiosyncrasies, but did I really want to drive that home? Give him more jokes to tell? Hmm. On second thought, it was probably a good idea. He would see how truly wrong we were for each other. And that I did the best thing for us when I left. Then he could go back to his famous life, and I could go back to my quiet and well-thought-out one. "I'll tell him as soon as he wakes up. I'm going to go for a walk now."

I needed to clear my head, and it was that time of day. Hal and Stu would worry if they didn't "see me like clockwork," as they would say. Plus, they might have more candidates for me to date. I was hoping to schedule two dates a week for a month, eliminating one man each week. Then the next month I would narrow it down again to two. Surely, out of eight men, I could fall in love with one of them. And vice versa. They did it all the time on *The Bachelorette*. I would admit to no one I watch that show occasionally, even though I kind of planned to do the same thing without the rose ceremony and hopefully without all the made-up drama.

"Call us later and let us know how it goes," Jolene said.

"Good luck," Tara added.

Who needed luck when you had what some would consider borderline unhealthy tendencies on your side? Jolene was right: telling Josh would send him running away screaming, thanking his lucky stars he didn't get stuck with me. The woman who scheduled *everything*. Was I still salty about his recent routine? Definitely.

Feeling good about this plan, I walked out of my

office/workout room—the only other room I had in the house besides my bedroom—and headed for the front door. When I turned the corner into the living area, I couldn't help but pause and stare at Josh sleeping so peacefully curled up under the quilt. I'd missed the way he would smile in his sleep like he was now. He had the best dreams. He used to love to share them with me as soon as he would wake up, which was usually several hours after I had been awake. I was an early bird, and he was a night owl. It was the nature of his job. Many of those dreams included me. Of course, a lot of them were steamy montages, but there were also the sweet ones. Ones of us swinging on the swings until we reached the leafy treetops. I loved to swing. Swinging by myself in the park while I was growing up was one of my only sources of entertainment. There was something so freeing about it. Josh had even once dreamed of us getting married and him somehow forgetting to wear clothes to the ceremony.

I wondered what he was dreaming about now. Did I still make my appearances? Part of me hoped he still dreamed of us going to the park and lying on a blanket to watch the clouds turn into stars. If only real life could be so lovely, so easy. But being with Josh was complicated. On one hand, when it was just Josh and me together, I had been freer to be myself than I ever had. But on the other hand, when we were on the road or even just around his crowd, I constantly felt like I needed to either pretend to be someone I wasn't or play the part of a social outcast when it got to be too much for me. I couldn't handle a lifetime of misery trying to be someone I wasn't.

I felt like that throughout my youth into adolescence—the invisible girl no one wished to befriend. Honestly, part of me had been glad. I feared if people got to know me, they would really see how weird I was. But deep down, I wanted someone, anyone, to just recognize I existed. No one but Nana seemed to until I met Tara and Jolene. Unfortunately, we didn't visit Nana often when I was growing up. My friends became the characters in the books I read in the library, where I spent nights and weekends.

All Josh's friends and acquaintances treated me like that invisible girl. Several of them wondered why Josh would date someone as awkward as me. I'd heard one guy say, "At least she's hot. I guess that's worth staying for."

I never told Josh about it. He already knew what people said about me. That he could do better. I really wanted to be the fun girl who could go with the flow. But life had taught me to be guarded. To be afraid of myself. After all, when the people who should love and support you the most think all you are is a burden, a klutz, chubby, ugly, you name it, it's hard not to want to hide from the world.

But for Josh, I tried to be the woman I thought he wanted, even needed. In the end, it got to be too much. Josh had told me he didn't want me to be anyone else but myself, that we could work it all out. But his life was only becoming more and more public. And the long separations were proving to be difficult for both of us.

I wasn't exactly sure why Josh came here, but if he had any inkling of us rekindling what we once had, it was best for me just to nip it in the bud. That road would only lead us right back to where we were now. Besides, I abhorred him, even if he looked adorably sexy sleeping on my couch. I longed to crawl under the covers with him and nestle right into his chest. Which was saying something, since it would obliterate what I had left on my schedule. But he was the king of getting me to do things outside my norm.

It's why I rushed toward the door and grabbed my jacket from off the hook. I couldn't afford to let the thought of letting Josh into my life again creep in. I once read that it's not so much how compatible you are but how you deal with incompatibility. Our incompatibilities were like crossing one of those ancient rope bridges across a body of water full of crocodiles—treacherous and not for the faint of heart. Especially not for someone who didn't wish to have viral videos of herself. Stupid man.

I walked out into the sunshine at ten sharp and let it warm my cheeks. I breathed in the cool morning air, trying to find my equilibrium. Not sure it was possible. I felt like I was back in junior high school with buck teeth and the most awful stage fright imaginable. Worse, I felt completely out of control. This was way more dreadful than my jam crisis brought on by the ridiculous grocery store management. The only thing I had going for me was that most of my neighbors were part of the geriatric crowd and weren't on social media. Hal and Stu believed it was the downfall of society. They weren't wrong. It was certainly going to add to my demise. It made me want to walk back into the house, except the reason for my consternation was in there.

Walk it was. I could at least control my routine.

As if someone were following me, I sped up my pace. I felt so on display. It kept the Josh hate burning. He had more than humiliated me. He was upending my life. And for what? *Because I stole everything from him.* Oh, that pricked my heart. If he only knew how much it hurt me to have done so. How much I loved him and haven't felt the same since we've been apart. But he could never know those things. Didn't he see how incompatible we were?

I shoved my chilly hands in my jacket pockets and hustled to the park. I had this need to pull my jacket hood over my head and hide, but I desperately didn't want to be that woman. How was I going to find love if I was hiding? I had survived the airport, and I was sure there were a couple of women who had pointed at me and murmured between themselves, probably about the video. I had almost left the gate to go rent a car and drive home, but I feared getting on some TSA watchlist. I survived it, just like I had every other embarrassment in my life. Alec always loved to point that out. He also loved to say, "Why are you giving strangers a say in how you feel about yourself?" Was that poignant? Sure. But putting it into practice was entirely different. Probably because the people who should have loved me mocked me the most growing up.

Sometimes I wondered if my parents were out there ridiculing me now. I hadn't talked to them since Nana died. My therapist helped me to see those were relationships that deserved endings with big fat periods that I should never erase. Especially after the vitriol they tossed my way when they learned Nana had left me all that she owned. That was a terrible time. Josh wasn't the only one who lost *everything*. Though I would never claim a complete loss. I still had Jolene and Tara. I had gained Hal and Stu. I supposed I better throw Alec in there, too.

For those who had stood by me, and for myself, I didn't cover my head. If worse came to worst, I would let Tara unleash some names to take off the heat. She was itching to anyway.

By the time I made it to the park, I was feeling pretty toasty, considering it was only in the forties. The fear of exposure really does something for your pace.

Hal and Stu were already there, eyes set at the entrance. As soon as they saw me, they jumped up. Well, *jump* is an exaggeration, but they moved faster than I had ever witnessed. Immediately, I worried something was wrong. Normally, they arrived after I'd started my way around the path. Then they took a seat to rest from the walk over.

I picked up the pace even more and met them. "Is everything okay?"

"Just fine, darlin'." Stu cleared his throat.

"How are *you*?" Hal asked with meaning.

I narrowed my eyes at them, ready to dig deeper, but then it dawned on me . . . "You heard about the video, didn't you?"

Stu gave me an uneasy smile. "Well . . . you see . . . my granddaughter might have mentioned something when she dropped by yesterday."

I hung my head and sighed. If my favorite social media-hating old men had heard about it, I was for sure moving out of the country. Maybe to a remote village without the internet. But then I could never secretly watch *The Bachelorette* again. That probably wasn't such a bad thing. That said, a place with no internet probably didn't have all the comforts of life I enjoyed, and I wouldn't be able to work. Ugh. I hated Josh.

"So that's Josh?" Stu laughed.

My head snapped up. "Yeah, that's him," I grumbled.

Hal chuckled. "Man must still have a thing for you. Should we put him on our list to interview?"

"No," I was quick to say. "He's actually at my house now."

Both of their brows flew to the sky.

"It's not what you think. After my walk, I plan to kick him out. Forever." That hurt to say, but it had to be said. I could not have a life of being in the spotlight. Especially when it wasn't all that flattering on me.

"Why did he come?" Hal asked.

"I'm not exactly sure. Something about unfinished business."

Stu pressed his lips together, trying not to smile. "Unfinished business, huh? Sounds kind of serious."

Hal looked to Stu, nodding. *"Very serious."*

I pinched the bridge of my nose. "I assure you, it's not. Besides, he disgraced me in public."

"Hmm," Hal said. "That we can't have."

"Should we come over and rough him up?" Stu asked.

I giggled. "I don't think that will be necessary."

Hal patted my cheek. "Are you okay, honey?"

I leaned into the affection. It was something Nana used to do. I missed her. Even though I had a feeling she would be thrilled Josh had shown up and would probably tell me not to kick him out. She used to say, "That boy is good for you." In many ways it was true, but how was this exposure good for me? "I'm working on it."

"Well good, because we have another man for you." Stu rubbed his hands together, showing he was getting down to business.

I bit my lip. "You do?"

"This is assuming Dr. Kristoff and you don't fall madly in love at first sight."

"That's not going to happen," I said skeptically, despite being pretty sure I had fallen in love with Josh on our first date. I'd never admitted that out loud. It was very unlike me. Regardless, I don't think you get that magic more than once. Hopefully, I would get some new magic. Like the non-famous kind.

Hal shrugged. "You never can tell about these things. I fell in love with Anna the first time I saw her in the audience at an old smoky bar."

"I remember that night," Stu reminisced fondly. "You left the stage before our set was done."

"I couldn't let her get away." Hal grinned.

"That's sweet."

"Looks like you had a bit of that over the weekend." Stu winked.

I cringed, thinking about it. "I'm sure Hal didn't announce Anna was a thief to a crowd of people." I had been lucky enough to meet Hal's wife not long before she passed. She was sassy as could be. I adored her. Sadly, I didn't have the opportunity to be acquainted with Stu's wife, Ruth. But I felt like I knew the women for as much as their husbands fondly spoke of them.

"Sometimes a man's got to do what a man's got to do to get the girl." Hal chuckled.

"I thought you were on my side."

"Honey, we are always on your side, but I can understand the desperation and stupidity of a man," Hal replied.

Josh was stupid. Cute, but stupid.

"So, who's the new guy?" I thought it best to change the subject.

"He's a hometown boy who just recently moved back. He's an actuary now."

That detail perked me up. Actuaries had been voted the most boring well-paid job in a recent business article I'd read doing research for one of my client's books. I liked it.

"Kyle is a good man, never been married, but he was engaged last year."

"Who broke it off?" I had to know.

"It was mutual," Stu responded.

"Huh. Do you know why?"

"Sure, sure," Hal said. "We wanted to be thorough. Kyle said she wanted more of a big-city life, and he likes small-town life."

Ooh. That was good. "How old is he?"

"Thirty-three. And he loves to run, has a credit score of 840, and he goes to church every Sunday," Stu bragged about the man.

He sounded better and better. "Let's set a date," I said as chipperly as possible, praying neither Kyle nor Seth had seen the video.

"Great." Hal clapped.

"I really appreciate all your help with my, uh . . . goal." That was a good word for it.

"Sure, sure. We're happy to help," Hal said. "We have a few more candidates to interview this week."

They had no idea how much that meant to me. "You guys really are the best." I got a little emotional.

"We just want to see you happy," Stu beamed. "You're like a daughter to us, Hepburn."

My eyes stung with tears. No one but Nana had treated me like a daughter before. Well, I guess Josh's parents were an exception, but I couldn't think about it. I wrapped my thin arms around both of them as best I could. "Thank you," my voice cracked.

They each gave me a squeeze.

"You're a good kid," Hal said, sounding very fatherly.

"You best get your walk in," Stu added.

Love Rescheduled

I leaned away, wiped my eyes, and nodded.
"Good luck kicking that fella out of your house," Stu said.
Oh, I didn't need luck. I had neurotic tendencies on my side.

Nine

I TIPTOED INTO MY HOUSE. Not sure why I was being so considerate of my unwelcome houseguest. Maybe because as much as I needed him to go, there was a part of me wishing he could stay forever. Except, that part of me was super humiliated and hated him for it. Go, he must.

I hung up my jacket with a deep sigh.

"Hi, honey. You're home," filled the air, startling me.

My heart beat out of control as I grabbed my chest and spun around. I found a disheveled Josh sitting up, running a hand through his mussed hair. "I'm not your honey."

"You used to like it when I called you that."

I stepped closer, glaring at him. "*Used to* being the keywords."

My ire didn't faze him one iota. "Do you like *sweetheart* better now? *Baby? Goddess divine?*"

I pressed my lips together, trying not to be taken in by his charm. "You need to go." Like right this minute, before I wanted to kiss him until he made me forget why we weren't right for each other.

"Hmm." He bounced a bit on the couch. "I don't know. This couch is pretty comfy. I'm going to pass."

I rubbed my forehead. "You can't just stay here. I didn't invite you, and I'm in the middle of an extensive project."

Love Rescheduled

"For work?"

"No."

He looked around at my pristinely clean house. "Home renovation?"

"No." I looked down at my feet as if that would give me some courage to tell him the crazy truth.

"So, what's this *extensive* project?"

I let out a heavy breath and raised my head.

Josh's smooth-as-chocolate eyes grabbed my own and refused to let go.

I swallowed hard. "The truth is, I'm getting married this fall."

Josh's face turned the color of a few-days-old corpse. Yes, I knew what that looked like. As an editor, you would not believe the things I had to research. I prayed the NSA wasn't studying my internet-browsing habits.

"You're engaged?" he could hardly say the words.

"No," I admitted.

His face contorted. "You just said you were getting married."

"I am." I walked past him to the kitchen to get some water before I went back to work.

Josh reached out and gently grabbed my arm on the way. Pain etched his features, making me feel guilty, but I couldn't retreat now, no matter how much his touch felt like home and happier days. "Nat, are you with someone?" he begged to know.

I shook my head, fearing if I opened my mouth, my heart would speak on my behalf.

He scrubbed his free hand over his stubbled cheeks. "I don't understand."

I pulled away from him, wrapping my arms around myself. "You don't need to understand. But I'm getting married in September."

"To whom?" he demanded to know.

I was proud of him for using correct grammar there, but I

didn't mention it. "I don't know yet. It's a work in progress." I scooted to the kitchen.

Josh jumped off the couch and followed me. "What do you mean 'it's a work in progress'?"

I opened the refrigerator. "I think that's pretty self-explanatory."

"Enlighten me," he said, flatly.

I grabbed my pre-made bottle of water with freshly squeezed lemon in it, not wishing to face him. But a girl had to do what she had to do. As much as it killed me, I had to rid myself of Josh. Someday he would thank me when he married a non-awkward, vivacious, lover-of-the-spotlight-who-didn't-schedule-everything kind of woman. Would I hate her? Probably. But I would be happy Josh was living his dreams with a compatible partner by his side.

I shut the refrigerator door, turned, and leaned against it, holding my water bottle for dear life.

Josh gripped a kitchen chair, intensely gazing at me, nonverbally demanding an answer.

Oh, I had one for him. Get ready for him to scream his way out of here. That gave me some pause, but then I thought of the video and remembered his life was no life for me. "The truth is, I want to get married before I turn thirty, so I scheduled a date, and now I'm dating a pool of highly qualified and vetted men to choose from."

His jaw dropped before he spluttered, looking for some words to say. When he finally found them, this came out of his mouth: "Are you serious? You think you can just schedule love and marriage?"

I pursed my lips together and thought. "Yes."

"Oh, hell." He rubbed the back of his neck. "Nat, you know that's not how it works, right?"

I pushed off the refrigerator. "How do you know?"

He stared at me blankly, no words forming.

That's what I thought. "I need to get back to work. You can

see yourself out." I sounded much braver than I felt. My heart was breaking. Like Nana would say, "Some of the hardest things you will ever do are the right things."

The infuriating man followed me back to my office. "The front door is the other way," I reminded him while I crossed the threshold, heading for my desk.

Josh leaned against the doorframe and watched me settle in at my neatly organized desk. Lord Mac was patiently waiting for me.

"Go already." I pointed, albeit shakily. I wasn't used to being so bold.

Josh folded his arms, showing he wasn't going anywhere. "Nat, you can't be serious about this."

"I assure you I am."

"What about us?"

"What about *us*?" I repeated, my voice wavering.

"At the club you said you still loved me," he said point-blank. "That means nothing to you?"

My eyes began stinging, fiercely, but I held back the emotion the best I could, knowing Josh would use it to his advantage. I couldn't risk us replaying the scene from three years ago, where he almost convinced me to stay. "Of course it means something to me. That will never change. But this"—I pointed between us—"this isn't a good idea. So, please go," I pleaded.

"No," he refused. "This is asinine. I let you convince me once we won't work. I'm not doing that again."

Oh, no, no, no. I couldn't let him fight for us. This was not part of the plan. "I don't think you needed much convincing, considering you got engaged five months after we broke up," I threw at him.

"You don't know what you're talking about. Ask anyone close to me."

"Camila, maybe? You two got awfully cozy. Did that start before or after we broke up?"

Josh's face turned a shade of red I didn't know was possible.

"Damn it, Nat, you know I never cheated on you. Never even thought about it. You're the one who walked out. Not me."

I couldn't contain my emotions. Tears filled my eyes, guilt consumed my soul, and an ache so deep pierced me and shattered my heart. "And you told me if I did, there was no coming back. So, why are you here?"

He dropped his arms along with his defenses. "Because for three years I've been kicking myself for not opening that door."

I didn't dare tell him I had watched and waited for the handle to turn. Or that I had begged myself over and over to walk back through the door. "You did the right thing," I said, half-heartedly.

"I don't think so, and deep down you don't either."

I sat up stiffly. "You're wrong. I did what was best for you and me."

He shook his head. "I don't believe that for one second, and neither do you."

"Will you please quit telling me what I do and don't believe? It's obvious we don't work. You blindsided me on Friday night, and now it's all over social media. Do you know what that's doing to me?"

He hung his head. "I know. I didn't know what to do. I thought I would never see you again, and there you were. I couldn't let you get away."

"If you wanted to talk, you know where I live. You could have even called."

"Well, I'm here now, so let's talk."

I knew talking would be futile. His life wasn't going to magically change, and neither was mine. "Josh, please go," I begged. "I have a schedule to keep here, and I have a date with a doctor on Wednesday."

"Does he know about your ridiculous plan?"

"Who says it's ridiculous?" Besides me. Alec had said sometimes the most ludicrous ideas have bettered humanity. Why not this one?

"Everyone."

I shrugged. "Well, there you have it. I'm a lunatic, so you best be off."

"I see what you're doing, and it won't work. I'm staying."

There were conflicting feelings coursing through me. A part of me loved that he still wanted me and was willing to fight for what we had lost. The other part of me was astonished and exasperated beyond belief at his tenacity. It's terrible manners to show up at your ex's house and invite yourself to stay. Especially when I had men to date and fall in love with. Josh was going to put a real damper on my plan. "Don't you need to get back to LA? I heard you're about to sign a big contract. Is that for a movie or TV show?"

The blood drained out of his face. "Who told you that?"

"Zac," I hissed his name. "He warned me not to screw it up. I have no intention of doing so."

"He shouldn't have said anything."

"Why? It doesn't change the reality of the situation. I'm proud of you, Josh. Except when you lambasted me and used me as a punchline. But sincerely, I am. You deserve all the good coming your way. It's what you've worked so hard for. So, go back to LA. Don't look back," my stupid voice hitched.

"I never want to see you in the rearview mirror again." He paused, I assumed for me to respond.

It rendered me speechless. What a beautiful thing to say, except he was supposed to leave me in the dust. The dust I had already swept away and made peace with.

"I'm going to go hop in the shower," he casually said, as if he hadn't just rocked my entire well-ordered world. "See you later, *honey*." He smirked before walking off.

Ugh. I rested my head on the desk, feeling all sorts of out of control. How dare the man still love me? This was supposed to be an unrequited love thing on my part. I planned it that way. And gosh darn it, it was going to stay that way. No famous men ever again.

ten

"ALEC, STOP LAUGHING. I'M PAYING you to help me, not find pleasure in the crazy events of my life." I had just explained the sticky situation I had going on over here. I was currently hiding in my bedroom listening to my ex sing "Love to Love You Baby" by Donna Summer in my kitchen while making his lunch. This was after he paraded around in nothing but a towel while throwing a load of his laundry in the washing machine. I *knew* his duffel bag was full of dirty clothes. Did I peek at his chest? Yes. Was it still beautiful with just the right amount of definition and dark hair? Also, yes.

Alec cleared his throat, trying to stop his fits of laughter, but his chuckles kept escaping. "I'm sorry; it's just . . . you can't make this stuff up." He wasn't wrong. Tara was going to get a lot of new material out of this for her next book. She and Jolene were going to die when I told them Josh was refusing to leave. I hadn't had the chance yet, as I couldn't believe this was happening to me.

"What do I do?" I whined while grabbing a pillow from my bed, where I had nestled myself. Josh was throwing my entire life into chaos. I was supposed to be at my kitchen table, where I always talked to Alec.

"Why are you asking me that question?" Alec tossed back at me. "The better question is, what do you want to do?"

"I want him to leave."

"Why do you want him to leave?"

"Isn't that obvious? We broke up and he made me a laughingstock over the weekend."

Alec cringed on the screen. "I saw the video."

I rolled my eyes. "Of course you did. Everyone's seen it."

"If it makes you feel better, most of the comments reflect poorly on him, not you."

"It doesn't make me feel better. I don't want anyone to make comments about my life online." Especially ones about how I scheduled intimacy. It wasn't that uncommon. Relationship therapists even recommend it sometimes.

"What have we talked about before? You have to be okay letting people be wrong about you."

I curled more into myself. I didn't love that advice. "Josh is wrong about me. We don't belong together."

"Then why are you so upset he's there?"

"I don't like these questions, Alec. You're supposed to just fix it already," I joked.

He chuckled. "You know that's not in my job description. I'm here to act as a guide to help you achieve your goals."

"My new goal is to kick Josh out."

"So, what's your plan?"

"My plan failed. I told him about my upcoming wedding, thinking it would do the trick, but that only seemed to make him more determined to stay. He doesn't believe I can schedule love."

"He might not be wrong."

I scrunched my nose. "I thought you said if anyone could do it, I could."

"I stand by that statement, but I also said it may not end in marriage."

Oh, it was going to just so I could prove Josh wrong. "Alec, I feel so out of control right now. I need your help. Like, desperately."

"Natalie, I think that's the root of your problem. You think you can control everything, but you can't. If I may say, I think you should honestly ask yourself why you left Josh. Was it because you preemptively wanted to control the outcome?"

"No," I spluttered, highly offended he would think such a thing. "I did it because I loved him enough to let him go. So he could live a happier, fuller life."

"But you can't control that. Did you ever stop to think that his life was happier and fuller with you in it?"

"It wasn't," I sighed. "I made him miserable."

"Then why is he there?"

"He loves being tortured?" I half laughed.

"Possibly, or maybe your insecurities stemming from your childhood clouded your vision. Maybe you listened to your parents' voices, not your own."

I blinked and blinked, not knowing what to say. That thought kind of hurt. Like a big ouchy.

Alec's face softened. "Or perhaps I'm entirely wrong."

"I don't want to live in the spotlight," was all I could think to say.

"That's understandable. Few people would."

Before I could respond, Mr. Spotlight barged in, carrying a plate full of food. "Hi, honey . . ."

Alec chuckled.

I glowered at Alec and then at Josh. "Excuse me, I'm in the middle of something." I nodded toward Lord Mac.

Josh didn't take the hint and walked toward the bed. "I noticed you didn't eat lunch, so I made your favorite egg, tomato, and avocado sandwich on whole-grain bread. Orange slices on the side."

That sounded good, but he didn't need to know that. "Thank you. You can put it on the nightstand."

Josh, being Josh, didn't listen to me. Instead, he hopped up on my bed, plate in hand, barely keeping the oranges from falling off the plate onto my white comforter. Yes, I had a lot of white in my house. It was easier to see if things were clean that way. Am I a clean freak? I think we all know the answer to that.

I grabbed the plate before he could spill it on my bed.

Josh zeroed in on Alec, his eyes narrowing. "Are you having a date in here?"

"Not that it's any of your business, but no. Alec is my life coach."

Josh's posture immediately relaxed. "Life coach. I like it. Nice to meet you, man." Josh scooted closer to me. Thankfully, he was fully dressed in jeans and an Eagles T-shirt. Sadly, he smelled too good.

"The pleasure is all mine." Alec could hardly contain his toothy grin.

"You can go now," I complained to Josh.

"I think I better stay. I probably need to defend myself."

Alec laughed but quickly stopped when I shot him a scathing glare. He was supposed to be on my side. I was the one paying him, after all.

"Alec is not my therapist, and this isn't couples therapy."

"Maybe we should give that a try." Josh nudged me.

I set the plate on my lap and groaned. How had this become my life?

"I'll take that as you're thinking about it." Josh laughed. "So, what does a life coach do?" Josh asked Alec.

"Uh, excuse me, I'm paying for this session."

"I'm going to give you this one on the house." Alec seemed overjoyed to do so before giving his attention to Josh. "I help people personally and professionally by encouraging them and counseling them through challenges to achieve their goals." He took that right off his website.

"Any profession?" Josh asked.

"Absolutely."

"Great, now that we cleared that up. You should go."

"I have a few more questions." Josh wasn't deterred. "Besides, you should eat. I know you've probably been too stressed to the last few days," he said so sweetly. "I apologize for that."

He knew me so well that I hated and loved him for it. He always liked to take care of me, and me him. It wasn't helping the situation at all. That little nugget Alec threw at me about my insecurities basically sabotaging our relationship didn't make me feel all warm and fuzzy either.

"Eat." Josh smiled. "Alec and I will get acquainted while you do."

I noticed Alec scribbling down a lot of notes. None of which better include things like, *This chick is crazy if she doesn't take this man back.* It's not like I didn't know that I was a little quirky, perhaps neurotic.

Josh grabbed Lord Mac and placed him on his lap. "When she gets overwhelmed, her appetite is the first to go," he informed Alec with the utmost concern in his freaking sexy, gravelly voice.

I was overwhelmed, thanks to him. And he was right. I had hardly eaten in the last few days. The sandwich looked good, and my stomach had been growling. I picked up half the sandwich Josh had cut diagonally, just how I like it. Might as well eat as my life coach and ex were getting chummy, talking about their favorite sports teams. Josh was a college football fan and loved Tennessee. Alec was more of a professional sports guy and loved the Celtics and Red Sox. It made sense, given he lived in Boston. One of my Boston clients had recommended him to me. Alec had helped him up his writing game.

I took a bite of the sandwich and savored it. For whatever reason, when Josh made them, they always tasted better. He used to say it was because he made them with love. He wasn't supposed to still love me. I thought I had fixed that. Alec was right. I tried to control that particular outcome. Obviously, I'd failed. But that didn't mean we should be together. I knew I would hold Josh back from his dreams, and eventually he would come to resent me. Or he would live his dreams and they would crush me. It was a no-win situation, then and now.

I ate and watched Josh easily converse with Alec like they'd known each other for years. I always admired that quality in him. He could make anyone his best friend. With each bite, my blood sugar levels thanked me. The headache I had dissipated.

I sighed in relief, and Josh glanced my way, smiling. "Feel better now?"

I nodded.

"Good. Now my job is done. It was good to meet you, Alec. I'll touch base with you soon. I look forward to working with you."

Wait. What? How did I miss that part of the conversation? "Alec is *my* life coach!" I sounded like a child who was refusing to share a toy.

"There is plenty of me to go around." Alec chortled.

"Besides, honey, I have a feeling I'm going to need a lot of relationship help in the coming days and weeks."

I narrowed my eyes at Josh. He better not be talking about us, but I was sure he was. "With Zac?"

Josh fake laughed. "She's so cute when she's sarcastic."

"I really abhor you right now."

"I'm glad to hear you say that. It's going to make the making up so much better." He wagged his brows while placing Lord Mac back in front of me.

I tried very hard not to think of all the make-up scenarios we had played out over our time together. He wasn't lying, though. The angrier we were at each other, the hotter the reconciliation seemed to be. That being the case, I could only imagine the cosmic levels of heat we would reach if we did indeed make up. But that wasn't going to happen, no matter how bad my body was begging for it. "You're insane."

"You flatter me." He kissed my cheek before hopping off the bed. "Talk to you later, man," he called out to Alec.

I touched my cheek, which sizzled from his touch. Then I

set my plate on the nightstand before facing a grinning Alec. "Girl, you're in trouble. That's off the record, of course."

"What do you mean?"

"You don't know? The man is obviously in love with you and determined to get you back."

I pulled my knees up to my chest. "It will never work."

"You know I hate the word *never*."

"Now you're taking his side?"

"Natalie, I'm always on your side. I want you to be happy and successful. But you need to ask yourself objectively where you will find your genuine joy. What does Natalie's voice say?"

I wasn't sure how to respond. I'd always had a hard time listening to my voice. Sometimes my voice was my worst critic. But was that truly my voice or my parents in disguise?

"You don't have to answer that now, but give it some serious thought. If Natalie could have her dream, what would that look like?"

Possibly a nightmare. "I'll think about it."

"Don't just think about it. Visualize it. Remember, you can't control anyone or everything, but you can redirect your thoughts and the way you think about yourself. I think you need to work harder on seeing yourself for who you truly are. Not who your parents or anyone else thinks you are. I have a feeling that might change the way you envision your present and future."

"Okay," I said quietly.

"And let me apologize for my unprofessional behavior today. I shouldn't have allowed for the disruption. Josh has a way about him, doesn't he?"

Wasn't that the truth.

Eleven

AT SIX, I TOOK A break from working. Well, more like staring at my screen. All the words seemed to be a blur. It was dinnertime, but I wasn't sure if I should emerge from my office. My houseguest was still lurking about. At least he had given me some space to work. Not that it had done me much good. All I could think about was Josh. He was determined to stay and wreak havoc on my life. Tara and Jolene suggested I just let him stay and watch me date other men. We were all still livid about him making me his punchline and the ongoing embarrassment. The video hadn't died yet. Tara was making a list of names to expose, just in case.

Their suggestion wasn't terrible, but we all knew how persuasive Josh could be.

Josh wasn't the only thing on my mind. I thought a lot about what Alec had said. I swore he was daring me to free myself from myself. To let go of others' opinions of me, especially my parents'. My therapist and I had discussed that for sessions on end. The key, she said, was to recognize that I actually have high self-esteem. She'd said I'd made too many good choices in my life for me not to. Many of which were brought on by a need to control my destiny. So how could control be that bad? Sure, I was lonely, and I had left the only man I ever loved, but I was a successful editor—freelance, of course, because who had time for office politics? Or people? Josh's life was very people-y.

And not to toot my own horn, but I had a retirement account and a rainy-day fund, and every month I chose a good cause to donate to. Not only that, but I was working toward adding relationships to my life. I was letting my favorite senior citizens set me up on blind dates. So, there was an interview process, but it was pretty noncontrolled if you asked me. Did I have an exit strategy planned for my upcoming date? Absolutely. However, in this day and age, that was just plain smart.

A knock on the door interrupted my contemplation. It was surprising Josh hadn't just barged in.

"Yes," I said, exasperated.

Josh peeked his cute head in. "Dinner's ready."

I had wondered what all the banging around was, but I thought it best just to leave Josh to his own devices. The less contact, the better. "You didn't have to make dinner."

"What kind of houseguest would I be if I didn't?"

"The kind that should leave."

"There you go with your jokes again." He smirked.

"Josh, this isn't a joke. You shouldn't be here."

"You say that now, but wait until you taste the chicken carbonara I made."

Ooh. I loved his carbonara. "The creamy kind?"

"Uh-huh."

I bit my lip.

"Come on. You know you're hungry and you're dying to catch up with me."

"I'm dying for you to leave."

He rolled his eyes, not falling for it. "I promise, this will be a *friendly* dinner. We haven't talked in three years. I want to know what's going on in your life."

"Well, let's see. I have this viral video going around where people make fun of my intimate habits. That about sums up my life right now."

Josh stepped all the way in and sighed. "Nat, I'm sorry I told that stupid joke. I'm even more sorry I broke my promise to you. It was just, I hadn't been home in a while and that place always reminds me of you. And the more I thought about you, the angrier I got."

"So it was a revenge joke."

"I never wanted revenge. I just wanted you back."

I rubbed my chest. The man was out to kill me for how much that pricked my heart.

"But we're not going to talk about that tonight. I just want to sit across the table from you and hear you tell me all about the new and fascinating facts you've looked up lately." That used to be part of our daily routine. As an editor, I was always having to verify information. Along the way, I had learned some pretty interesting things. It just kind of became a hobby to look up weird facts. I used to love to relay any new things I had learned over dinner or anytime we were together.

When I didn't say anything, Josh added, "I swear to you, I'll never use you in a routine again."

"Because of you, everyone thinks I'm a cold and sterile psycho."

"What the hell do they know?" he spewed, like it wasn't him who had given the world that impression of me. "Any man would be so lucky to see exactly how warm and tender you are. They would never be able to get enough of you."

His words made my cheeks burn. I jumped up. "Let's eat." Anything but talk about my favorite hour of the day. I could have that with someone else, right? Someone not famous.

Josh's eyes roved all over my body as I approached him. I knew exactly what he was thinking, but thankfully, he kept it to himself. My heart was already having too many palpitations.

"Nat," he said softly, "I hope you can forgive me someday. I know how hard it is for you to have people talking about you."

"I think that's what hurts the most. You know that better than anyone, yet you used me to get some cheap laughs."

"I didn't know you were there or that people would think it was about you."

"That shouldn't have mattered."

"You're right. If I could go back and do that night over, I would. I'm sorry my career once again caused you to feel unsafe and vulnerable. Do you know how much I hate that?"

That was exactly how I felt. He still knew me so well. If only he knew how much I wished I could feel safe in my skin. Maybe then things could be different. "Why do you think I left? You should never hate something you love so much."

Josh let out a heavy breath and ran a hand over his mussed hair.

In his eyes, I saw the turmoil a life with me caused. I'd seen it before.

"Yeah. Anyway, let's eat." Maybe he was finally seeing the light. Our worlds were too far apart.

We walked silently toward the kitchen. I had to stop and grip the wall when my small-but-functional, normally spotless kitchen came into view. Every pot and pan I owned was in various places, food splattered on them and the butcher-block countertops Nana adored. She was so proud when she'd saved enough money to have them installed. There were even specks of food on my cupboards. White cupboards painted by yours truly.

"What did you do in here?" I don't know why it surprised me. Josh was not the cleanest of men. Sure, he showered every day and brushed his teeth, but other than that, he was a slob.

Josh had the decency to look abashed. "You know how I get when I cook."

Oh, I knew.

"Don't worry, I'll clean it up." He grabbed my hand. "Come on, Nat, you can deal with this for a few hours."

"A few hours?" I scrunched my nose, itching to grab every disinfectant I owned and do some rage cleaning. I could do with a good rage clean. There was something about it that settled my soul.

"I think it's going to take a while for us to catch up." He squeezed my hand, then let it go before either of us got comfortable with the affection. I was grateful for that, seeing as my hand felt right at home in his.

"Fine," I half complained. It's not like my life wasn't already a hot mess of chaos. And I was hungry. "But the food better be amazing." That was not to say I was going to give him a few hours of my time tonight. I knew what happened when we talked for hours on end. And I don't mean a dirty kitchen. No, it was something much more beautiful. Too beautiful for me to allow to happen.

"Do you doubt me?" he asked with an air of sexiness no ex should use on you.

I cleared my throat. I never doubted him—only myself.

Josh took that as his cue to pull out a chair for me at Nana's old kitchen table. It had a Formica top with brass legs. I'd found some great retro chairs to go around it. It wasn't really my style, but around that table I had learned someone loved me. When I'd graduated from high school, I came running to Nana's. Every morning she would make me breakfast, usually grits with milk and sugar and a lot of butter. We would sit at that table, and she would do her best to make me believe in myself. I wished she were still here. I missed her now more than ever. Even if I knew she would tell me to give Josh another chance. "Let love find a way," she would say, even though her own love story was tragic and tumultuous. I only knew a little about her and my grandfather's relationship. It was obvious she was embarrassed to talk about the way he had treated her. More so that she had let him get away with it.

I took a seat and looked at the spread in front of me. Carbonara, salad, my favorite cranberry spritzer. Josh had even used Nana's old pink Depression glass plates. She would be so pleased. I glanced up at Josh, who was pushing in my chair. "This looks great. I never cook like this for myself."

"Me either." He sounded as lonely as I was.

It surprised me, considering all his social media posts. He was always with crowds of people, especially women. I had just assumed he was dating someone.

Josh took his seat across from me, a boyish smile on his face, making his dimples appear. "Before I forget to tell you, my parents wanted me to say hello and that they miss you."

"They do?" I figured they probably hated me along with everyone else close to Josh. The thought bothered me over the years, as I loved Laney and Kent. They had treated me like an actual daughter. Laney would always apologize to me for raising a slob.

"Of course. They always loved you."

"I just assumed . . ." I stopped short. I didn't want to rehash what had happened three years ago.

"They understood why," Josh hastily responded like he didn't wish to delve into it either.

"Were you visiting them? Is that why you were home?" I tried to redirect the conversation while serving myself a helping of carbonara.

Josh reached for his glass. "Part of the reason."

"What's the other part?"

He thought for a moment. "I just needed to clear my head. Take a country drive in my old truck."

"It surprised me to see Felicia in the driveway this morning." That's what Josh had named the old Chevy Silverado he'd driven since well before we'd met.

"Did you think I would go all city?"

I picked up my fork to dive into the cheesy pasta goodness on my plate. "Maybe. Do you like LA?"

He shrugged. "It has its perks, but it's . . . well, let's just say it's not home."

"But you're buying a place there?" I let slip out. Dang it.

Josh's face broke out in the smirkiest smirk ever. "Are you still following me on social media?"

"Why would I do that?" I refused to tell the truth. "I could have heard that from Jolene."

"You could have, but you didn't," he sang arrogantly. "It's fine. You don't have to admit it, but just so you know, I listen to your podcast every month."

I stopped twirling my pasta. "You do?"

"Yeah. You ladies have a good vibe going. You could really take it places if you wanted to."

I couldn't believe he was listening to our *A Party of Two and the Wallflower* podcast. "Of course, Jolene and Tara would love to expand our listener base, but you know me. I would rather not." I met his eyes so there would be no doubt about what I was trying to say to him. "I'm always holding people back. It's a gift." A crappy one, but a talent of mine nonetheless. I told Jolene and Tara to drop me from it and get a new introvert. It's not like we used my name or picture. That was kind of our shtick. Our cover photo was of them all dolled up in party clothes and I'm sitting there in sweats with a book covering my entire face. It's a running joke on the show that no one knows my name. They just say things like, *"Let's defer to our wallflower"* or *"The introvert says..."*

Josh's eyes bored right back into mine. "The only person you ever hold back is yourself."

I dropped my fork. "I excel at that." I couldn't hide the hurt in my voice despite wholeheartedly agreeing with him.

"I'm sorry, Nat. That was harsh."

"It's true, though. I know I hold others back, too, but you're right, I hold myself back the most. But I'm working on it."

He leaned in. "I know you never wanted to think of yourself as a victim, but you are. How your parents treated you is unforgivable. Yet, you turned out to be an amazing person despite it all."

More than anything, I hated feeling like a victim. It never

even struck home with me that I was until I went to therapy and they made me fill out the ACEs questionnaire measuring childhood trauma. I could answer seven out of ten questions in the affirmative. I won't lie, it was a bit triggering to see it on paper like that. It was the first time I even allowed myself to think I had been a victim. "I'm not amazing," I choked out.

"Yes, you are. You are the most incredible person I have ever met."

Right. He was constantly meeting fascinating and fantastic people. People who had achieved greatness like himself. "You're a good liar."

"I'm not lying. I've always been in awe of what you've overcome. I just hate to see that every minute you don't live the life you truly want, you let your parents continue to victimize you."

I blinked, stunned. That might have been the most poignant thing anyone had ever said to me. As in, why didn't my therapist ever say that to me in the two years I had been seeing her? Like honestly, wow. Just wow. Was I letting my parents revictimize me? Regardless, I didn't want a life in the spotlight. And I would never ask Josh to give up who he is just so we could be together. Believe me, I'd thought about it, but I knew it would never lead to good places. I never wanted to be selfish like that. With all that said, Josh's revelation made me more determined to not let my parents have a say in my life. I was going to have the life my mother and father had withheld from me. I was going to create a loving home with a husband and children and possibly a slightly neurotic wife and mother who only had their best intentions at heart. That meant I had to give more credence to my voice, rather than those of my parents.

Josh tilted his head. "What's that spark in your eye?"

"I was just thinking you should have been a therapist." And some other things I couldn't say to him. Like I was planning on marrying someone else. I couldn't hurt him like that at that moment. Even if he had thrust me into the spotlight over the weekend and the mortification appeared to be ongoing.

His beautiful eyes lit up. "So, you agree with my assessment?"

"I do. Thank you." I picked up my fork, already twirled with pasta, and took a bite. Mmm. Just like I remembered. The man was a wizard with parmesan cheese.

"I'm glad," he said, relieved. "So, tell me some new fascinating facts." He dug into his food.

I swallowed and thought for a moment. I couldn't explain how happy it made me he'd asked. No one else seemed to care for my vast, ridiculous knowledge. I made a mental note to make sure I shared a few facts on each date to gauge the man's interest. It was important to me that he enjoy that aspect of me. "Did you know no one knows how William Shakespeare's name is really spelled? Not even he knew. Funny, huh?" At least, I thought it was hilarious. Especially since the common spelling today is not one the world-famous playwright penned himself. I'd come across that tidbit researching a historical fiction novel for a client.

Josh flashed me a close-lipped smile as he chewed his food.

"Oh, did you also know that during the Industrial Revolution, there was an actual profession referred to as a *knocker-upper*?"

Josh spat out a laugh. "Is that like a male prostitute?"

"No. It was a person who would literally go around and knock on your door with a wooden stick to wake you up because most people didn't have alarm clocks back then. Sometimes they would even shoot peas at windows on the top floor."

"That's quite the wake-up call."

I smiled and grabbed my drink.

Josh watched my every move with a look of contentment. "Feels like old times."

Yeah, it did. Too bad I knew it would never last.

twelve

I LOOKED UP FROM MY laptop. Loud music was blaring in the bathroom, drowning out Horacio Gutiérrez's concerto performance I was playing in the background while I worked. Grrr. Josh. I thought he would be gone by now, especially considering I had a date tonight and yesterday we had a little tiff about him using my razor and leaving hair all over the sink. And . . . he'd helped himself to my expensive shampoo and conditioner. The man made more money than anyone I knew, and he couldn't pack his own toiletry bag? Don't even get me going on his clothes that were strung everywhere. It didn't matter how many times I picked them up and put them in the laundry basket I had given him; they seemed to multiply like gremlins when you watered them at night, and then they were wreaking destruction on my well-ordered, clean life.

I had gotten tough with Josh yesterday and told him we weren't getting back together, and I planned on keeping my dates with the doctor and the actuary this week. According to Hal and Stu, Kyle, the actuary, was excited to meet me this weekend. Kyle had apparently expressed that I sounded like the perfect woman for him. Josh only smiled and shrugged when I'd made my declaration. It was maddening. I was expecting him to say something snarky, or at least contrary, so we could argue about it, but no.

Regardless, whatever his game plan was, it wasn't going to work.

I pushed back my chair and marched over to the bathroom to the tune of Josh's morning song, "Da Ya Think I'm Sexy?" Oh, I was thinking some things about him, and it wasn't that he was sexy. I was going with *insufferable*. I pounded on the solid wood door, hurting my hand a bit. "Josh!"

He whipped the door open so fast it was like he had lured me there with his loud music on purpose. There he stood in all his glory with only a towel wrapped around his waist. A towel on the shorter side, mind you. He pointed at me and showed his alluring grin. "If you want my body and you think I'm sexy, come on, sugar, let me know." He wagged his brows, knowing exactly what he was doing. This was a trap. And it was working.

I stood immobilized, staring at his beautiful chest. Strong memories of how it felt to curl my fingers right into it were front and center in my mind. Or how safe I felt when my head landed in the soft forest of hair to hear Josh's contented heart beating only for me. And could we take a minute to appreciate his abs, which were even more defined? The boy had been working out. My hands itched to reach out and touch him. My mouth wished to utter that, oh yes, I wanted his body, and I thought he was sexy. That's when I did the sane thing and turned around.

Josh laughed loudly over his ridiculous get-ready song. "Come on, Nat, you know you want a piece of this. Dance with me, girl. I know you can. Remember that time on the tour bus when it was just us, and you said you always wished you had learned how to dance, and I showed you all the moves?"

Did I ever. A heat like the dead star in the center of the Red Spider Nebula consumed me, thinking of how sensual those dance lessons ended up being. When Josh wanted to, he could go well beyond silly dance moves. To his chagrin, his mother had made him take ballroom dance lessons as a teen. He must have been an excellent pupil. I closed my eyes, doing my best not to relive every second of the gorgeous memory of Josh sharing all his knowledge on the subject with me.

"Josh, please," I pleaded. "I need to work." Really, I needed to be submerged into an ice bath, but he didn't need to know that. That would have brought him far too much satisfaction. And I still kind of sort of abhorred him. Obviously, not enough to call the police to remove his half-naked self, but it still existed on some small level. It's a tad hard to hate someone who rubs your feet while you watch your allotted nightly hour of TV. I had almost begged him to rub more, which was exactly what he had wanted despite his no-strings-attached promise. Thankfully, I'd found the will to resist all the strings.

"Still distracted by my good looks?" he asked with an air of cockiness only he could muster.

"Just put some pants on," I responded, flustered. "And turn down the music. Maybe go home," I added. Not as emphatically as I should have. There lay my problem. All my attempts to throw his tight butt out were half-hearted. He knew it and I knew it. I was banking on him being turned off by everything about me that made us incompatible. Or, you know, the fact that I planned on marrying someone who wasn't him later this fall. I thought for sure that would have sent him packing.

Josh turned down the music until it was only humming in the background. "Home is such a relative term. Don't you think?"

"It depends on what you're comparing it to," I challenged him.

He grabbed my hand and spun me around before I could react to what he was doing. That's how I found myself peering right into the chest I longed to snuggle into, breathing in his freshly showered scent with a hint of lingering Obsession for Men. It was an amazing combo. Desire rose in me like hot molten lava ready to burst through the earth's crust, holding back its destructive power. A crack in the rocky layer broke when my head tilted up and my gaze landed on his lips, parted just enough to let me know he was inviting me to taste them. It was a miracle on his part and mine that our lips had not already collided in some glorious fashion after spending so much time together over the last couple of days. It's not that I hadn't thought about it on repeat, but I couldn't lead him on, knowing it would only hurt more when he finally departed.

Josh firmly gripped the hand he held. He raised his free hand and acted as if he were going to rest it on my cheek but instead only hovered over it as if he, too, were afraid to deepen our connection.

I remained still, hardly able to breathe, wondering if this is where I broke and gave in to the temptation to lean into his hand and let his lips consume mine until I forgot for a moment why we shouldn't be together.

His hand gently landed on my cheek, and his thumb immediately began caressing my smooth skin, leaving ripples of heat. "Didn't we used to say wherever we were together, that's where home is?"

We did. And in theory, it's a lovely thought. Even in practice, it was true. Josh is home. But his life was disquieting.

I swallowed down the lump in my throat, warring within myself whether to crush him or to love him, even if it would only lead to a worse ending than before. The battle raged and raged while my heart pounded relentlessly, not knowing whether it wished to break now or later. But then I remembered the utter hatred in Josh's eyes before I had turned and walked away for what I thought was the last time. I couldn't put either of us through that again.

"Josh, you are . . . well . . . I guess what I'm trying to say is, I love living in this small town and even in Nana's tiny cottage. I enjoy knowing I can go to sleep in my bed every night and wake up in the same place each morning. And here I'm free just to be my own quirky self instead of a freak on display."

Josh dropped his hand and mine, knowing where this was going. "I get it. You hate my life."

I felt terrible hurting him. "I don't hate your life. You have a great life, and you should live it to its fullest, like you're meant to do. It's just not a life meant for me." I said it all as bravely as I could, though inside, I was withering. I made myself play that stupid video from Laugh on Tap over and over in my head to remind me why this had to be.

"Yeah, so you keep saying." He ran his fingers through his hair, obviously unhappy.

"I'll let you finish getting ready. I'm going to go walk." Even though it wasn't ten yet. I just needed to get away from him and the hurt. I had to clear my head if I could.

"I thought you said you walked at ten every day." He'd asked about my schedule yesterday. I was sure he wasn't a fan of my rigid lifestyle. I hoped it brought him some comfort to know he wasn't going to get stuck with me and my routine.

"I do," I stuttered, backing away from him. Despite what was coming out of my mouth, every cell in my body was screaming for me to tackle him and prove to him I didn't schedule *everything*. I had never tackled anyone, so I wasn't sure where this thought was coming from or how to even go about accomplishing it. But a tiny voice inside me told me I could if only I would set myself free. It must be related to Alec. I took another step away from Josh, afraid of the voice, terrified of who I might become if I let go. I had to remind myself that engaging with Josh physically on any level was just cruel and unusual punishment. I would never toy with his feelings like that.

Josh tilted his head, looking concerned about the way I was stepping away from him. "I got up early so I could go with you."

I had wondered what he was doing up before noon. "Oh. Um. Well. You didn't have to do that."

His face tinged red. That wasn't the answer he was looking for. "There are a lot of things I don't have to do, but I want to do them. Funny how that works. Did you know you can do things just because you want to? Maybe you should try it sometime." He shut the door in my face.

I stood there in the throes of his rebuke, trying to think of a clever response, but nothing was coming to me except for how angry I was at him for being right. "Yeah, well . . . some people want to stab other people; it doesn't mean they should." I raised my voice, wishing I hadn't for how weak my retort was.

"That was lame, Nat, and you know it."

I hung my head in shame but determined to come up with the ultimate response that would prove to him that just because you want something, doesn't mean it's right. Hopefully, something would come to me on my walk.

I turned to go, feeling deflated and defeated. Was I just holding myself back again? Probably. But it was for a noble reason, right?

"By the way, you're not a freak," Josh yelled out.

I stopped and turned around. "What?"

He opened the door a crack and peeked his head out. "Earlier in our conversation, you said you were a freak on display. You're not a freak, Nat. You're a victim of your childhood."

There was that word again—*victim*. I hated it. My eyes stung with tears.

"I know you don't want to believe it, but that's what you are. It's made you who you are. An incredible woman who has some unhealthy coping skills."

My jaw dropped at the insinuation. I wouldn't exactly call them unhealthy.

"Don't look at me like that. Deep down, you know it's true. Natalie," he sighed, "the best times in my life have been when you allowed yourself to let go, even if it was just for a moment. If I were a betting man, and you know I am, I would say they were your best times, too." He flashed me a sly grin. "Remember that time we went with my parents to their cabin in Gatlinburg? And there were no schedules? Just day in and day out of us sleeping in until we wanted to and then playing games and exploring the town and mountains. How about our secret jaunts into the river at night?" he said as seductively as he could.

Oh, I remembered it all, and it showed in my burning cheeks.

"Nat, you can't tell me you weren't happy during that week."

It was the happiest I had ever been. But . . . "That was a vacation."

"A spontaneous one," he added.

True. But I had some other lame excuses to throw out there. "One where everyone recognized you and stopped us wherever we went," I grumbled.

Josh let out an exasperated breath. "You're just grasping at straws now. You didn't once complain that week. You know why?" He didn't give me time to answer. Not that I could have, anyway. I don't know why it didn't bother me that week. "I'll tell you why. It's because you were yourself that week."

I scrunched my nose. "I'm always myself."

"That's not true. You like to hide behind your schedules and insecurities, but that's not really you."

I faltered, feeling as if I'd been sprayed in the face with a hefty dose of cold water. He was saying things I didn't entirely appreciate.

His features softened, knowing he was causing me serious turmoil. "That's not to say I don't understand why you do what you do. But at least be honest with yourself. Have fun on your walk." He shut the door on me in more ways than one.

I should have been relieved he was finally seeing the light that was revealing just how much we didn't belong together. But all I felt was alone in the dark.

thirteen

I LOOKED AT MYSELF IN Nana's old oval standing mirror. The wood needed to be sanded down and refinished. It's kind of how I felt staring at myself in a fitted black jacket that accentuated my waist and slim black ankle pants. I was dressed more for a boardroom than a date. I had a playful jumpsuit with wide legs and ruffled cap sleeves hanging in the closet; I had bought it a year ago when I went shopping with Tara and Jolene. They had convinced me it was calling my name and if I didn't buy it, it would be a tragedy. It looked amazing on me, but I couldn't bring myself to wear the attention-grabbing outfit even though it rocked all my curves and said I was fun. That's the thing, though; I wasn't a "fun" person. I was the sensible designated driver person. The person who kept track of how many drinks Tara and Jolene had and, based on their weight and how much they had eaten, let them know what their blood alcohol level was. Why they were still friends with me, I didn't know.

Just like I had no idea why Josh was still here. We hadn't talked since this morning. As far as I knew, he'd hung out on the couch all day and watched TV. I think he was pouting. Meanwhile, I'd tried to work but kept getting distracted by his accusation that I wasn't honest with myself. I wasn't sure that was a fair assessment. I readily admitted I was quirky, possibly neurotic at times. How many people would own up to such a thing? Josh was crazy to think that some carefree woman lived inside this uptight control freak. That being said, I knew I needed to loosen up a bit. And I was trying. For crying out loud, I was going on a blind date, and I was trying to schedule love. If that wasn't progress, I didn't know what was. I was trying to free myself in the ways I could.

I debated on whether I should change into the jumpsuit, but when I stared into the mirror, all I could see was my red hair that inherently drew enough attention. Then I nitpicked how my teeth had shifted slightly despite the permanent retainer that should have prevented such a possibility. Or that my right eyelashes always seemed fuller than my left eyelashes. I could hear Alec screaming at me how important it is to speak kindly to oneself and to jump off this negative train as quickly as possible. But the train was speeding down the tracks, and I was afraid to jump off.

I stayed in the boring pantsuit.

Thoughts of canceling the date began creeping in like a warm and fuzzy friend who pretended to love me but, in reality, was my worst enemy. She wouldn't thwart me. There was no way I was going to tell Josh I was canceling. He was going to see he needed to find another Camila, no matter how much I hated the thought. She was like Gatlinburg Natalie all the time, except sexier and funnier. Oh geez, I just needed to leave before I hopped on the Camila train again. It always ended in a fiery crash of self-loathing. Choo choo.

Before I changed my mind, I grabbed my bag and ran out the door. I was tired of being lonely, and I was the queen of schedules. I could do this. I just needed to skirt past my ex. Ugh.

The clicking of my stupid heels against the hardwood floors alerted Josh to my presence before I had a chance to brace myself.

He sat up from his mopey lying-on-the-couch position. He had been staring aimlessly at the TV while his favorite show,

Ridiculousness, which was basically a panel of people watching stupid viral videos and making fun of them, filled the room with noise. It was Josh's dream to be a guest panelist one day.

"I'm leaving," I rushed to say. "There's food in the refrigerator. Goodbye."

"Wait." His eyes roved over me. "You look great." He didn't sound pleased about it.

"I look boring, but thanks." I started to leave again.

He did another take. "I don't know why you're always so down on yourself. Nothing you wear could ever be boring on that body of yours."

I bit my lip, thinking it probably wasn't good that I wanted to kiss Josh for his sweet comment, seeing as I was going on a date with another man.

"I never understood why you wanted to be like everyone else. There's a quiet confidence about you."

"Me? Confident?" I laughed.

"Laugh all you want, but the fact that you don't follow the crowd says a lot about you."

I wanted to believe him. Even more, I had this urge to stay home with him and cuddle on the couch. "I need to go." Like now.

"Don't you think you should tell me where you're going?" Was he for real?

"No."

"Aren't you worried at all? This guy could be a serial killer."

Of course I was. That's why I did one of those online background checks on him. Not to say I wasn't still worried. Honestly, I asked myself that about almost everyone I met, even Josh in the beginning. "That's why I told Jolene and Tara where I'm going to be. And I'm meeting him there."

"They're hours away. What good will they do you?"

"What good would anyone do if he's really a serial killer?" The thought made me queasy. Maybe I should just stay home.

"How many documentaries have we watched together

about this very subject? They don't usually kill their victims right away."

We were obsessed with watching them when we were dating. It was a morbid curiosity to be sure. But many psychologists believe it's because it represents the human condition, complete with heroes and villains, so it wasn't actually a psycho thing to do.

"True, but how would you find me?" I posed an important question.

His soulful chocolate eyes bored into mine. "I'd find you, Nat."

I believed him—heart and soul. "Fine. I'll be at Café Des Artistes. His name is Seth Kristoff. Do not—I repeat—do not show up."

He faux stabbed a knife into his chest. "Why would I do that? Do you think I want to see you on a date with another man?"

"I guess not."

"Here's a news flash: I don't. Try to find out the make and model of the car he drives and then text me."

"I'm not going to text you while I'm on a date."

"Go to the bathroom and do it."

"No. That would mean leaving my drink unattended, and what if he slips me something?" He was a doctor, after all. I had way overthought this. I was about to overthink myself right out of it.

"Good point. Keep an eye on your drink at all times. And whatever you do, don't go home with him," he stressed emphatically.

I rolled my eyes. "Does that sound like me?"

"You came home with me." He wagged his brows.

I cleared my throat. I still can't believe I had. But in my defense, we'd been flirting via DMs for a month before we ever went out, and Jolene and Tara thought he was a good guy. Not to mention we had spent all night together talking at a dive of a restaurant. "We only watched a movie."

"Liar. Your lips were all over mine."

"We are not having this conversation. I'm leaving."

"Don't be embarrassed. I totally dug it."

I wasn't embarrassed. I just couldn't think about the ... Best. First. Date. Ever. Longest, too. Now I was thinking about it all. I stared at his lips and thought about our first kiss. He'd asked me if I wanted a mint. When I replied yes, he popped one into his mouth and said, "Come and get it." We shared that mint back and forth until there was nothing left of it. I really had to stop thinking about it.

"Goodbye." I waved and rushed toward the door before I went and found my stash of mints and asked Josh if he wanted to play.

"Have fun," he sang in an abnormally cheerful tone.

I closed the door and wondered why Josh hadn't tried to talk me out of going. I'd thought for sure he would. Maybe he was finally getting the picture. I was going to title the work of art *A Lost Cause*. How depressing.

In the dark, I headed for my high-safety-rated Toyota Highlander under the carport. Sadly, the cottage didn't have a garage. I did my best not to look at Josh's truck in front of the house. A lot of beautiful things had occurred in its cab. *Not thinking about it. Not thinking about it.*

I hustled to the car, the damp cold seeping through me. I had forgotten to grab my coat, but no way was I going back into the house. There was no turning back now.

I sat in the parking lot of the restaurant, gawking at the stone building. Not shockingly, my confidence was waning. This was way, way, way out of my comfort zone. Alec would say nothing amazing ever happened in the comfort zone. He had never made out with Josh in his pj's; it was oh, so comfortable and amazing. So that theory was a lie.

Okay. Okay. I could do this. I'd set the wedding date, and I needed a groom. For all I knew, the Henry Cavill look-alike was going to blow Josh out of the water. All I had to do was walk in there and find out. I thought about the viral video of me and opened the door. Not to worry: if anyone in the restaurant recognized me, I had plans to turn right around and flee to Paris.

Thankfully, or sadly, depending on how you looked at it, there was a fresh scandal making its rounds in the comedian world. Chase Olson, the despicable human being whom Jolene had filled in for as headliner, apparently didn't have laryngitis. He had an acute case of jerk-itis. He was caught in a compromising position with another comic's wife in a Waffle House bathroom. Ew. That video was doing circles around mine. And everyone was buzzing about the war of words online between Chase and the jilted husband. I was hoping this meant I was old news. Don't get me wrong, I felt terrible for the husband. I even had a little sympathy for Tara. It bummed her out that she didn't need to release her list of names.

To calm my nerves, I mentally counted every step I took to get into the restaurant. I hadn't been on a first date in five years. *Not thinking of Josh or that perfect date.*

I finally made it to the entrance under a cute striped awning when I heard, "Hello, are you Natalie?" I turned to find the handsome doctor walking my way carrying a single white rose. He was wearing an impressive pair of jeans paired with a button-up and suit coat. Oh, wow. Move over, Clark Kent. Dr. Kristoff is in town. Josh only wore suit coats if he had to attend a funeral. Even then, he still wore a T-shirt under it. All not ironed, I might add. Why was I thinking about that? I needed to focus on how attractively the well-dressed man was smiling at me, presumably pleased with what he saw.

"I am Natalie," I responded nervously.

"It's so nice to meet you." His ice-blue eyes grabbed hold of me. It wasn't bad. No shivers or even a butterfly in my stomach, but I didn't detest it. That was something, right?

I clasped my hands together. This was getting all too real. "It's nice to meet you as well." I tried my best to sound natural.

He held out the rose to me. "I'm Seth, by the way, but you can call me Dr. Kristoff."

I wasn't sure how to respond. I was pretty sure he was joking. If he wasn't, this was going to be a quick night. No way was I calling him that.

"Just a little doctor's humor," he added.

"Oh, ha ha," I responded awkwardly. I was such a dolt. So much of one that I forgot to take the rose and he had to practically push it on me. I grabbed it and let out a huge breath. "I'm nervous," I blurted the cringeworthy truth. Why couldn't I just act fun and flirty?

Seth flashed me a smile. "I am too."

"Oh, good." Did I really just say that? Was I going to think that after everything I said tonight? Probably. I was remembering why I didn't date. Sure, being heartbroken was a big part of it, but dating made me a self-conscious ball of nerves. Except once. Somehow, Josh instinctively knew how to ease me through it all. You know, unless he was thoroughly embarrassing me. Or when his public life made me want to vomit.

Seth laughed, making me feel better. "Shall we do this?"

I breathed in the scent of the lovely rose, staring at the truly handsome man who had told Stu he came home every night around the same time and had most weekends off. And according to the background check, he had never been arrested. It was a good start.

"Yes, we shall."

fourteen

"So, you're an editor. What kind of books do you edit?" Seth was good at keeping the small talk going while we waited for our food. We sat in one of the handful of booths offered in the quaint restaurant with brick walls and colorful umbrellas hanging from the ceiling. I had ordered the boeuf bourguignon. It was the ultimate comfort food, and I needed as much comfort as I could get.

"Mainly fiction novels. My clients write in a wide range of genres."

"Which one is your favorite?"

"Well, considering one of my best friends writes rom-coms, I'm obligated to choose that one." I smiled. But Regency was my truest love. I kept trying to convince Tara to write in that genre. Honestly, though, I loved rom-coms. Probably because they gave me hope I wasn't the only person who continually found herself in awkward situations causing mass embarrassment. And they were the only romance I'd experienced over the last few years. Unless you counted my love affair with Lord Mac.

"I like a good rom-com." He took a sip of the wine he'd ordered.

I decided against drinking any alcohol. I wasn't a big fan in the first place, and there was no way I was risking being incapacitated in any shape or form.

"Really?" Josh loved them too. Ugh. I had to stop comparing Seth to Josh.

Seth set his glass down. "I have three older sisters I shared a bathroom with, so I basically lived in a rom-com."

"That's fun. I'm an only child." So was Josh. *Seriously, stop.*

"Do you feel you missed out?"

"I suppose so." I had missed out on a lot of things, but I didn't mention it. I felt it best to ease him into the dysfunction that was my family. First, we would have to see how he handled my quirks. That said, I was thankful my parents didn't have any more children. No child should have grown up in the environment I had.

Seth grabbed a piece of complimentary ficelle bread placed neatly in a basket between us. "You will never know the true joy of having four mothers," he said with an air of sarcasm.

Thank goodness for that. The one I had was awful. "Do you live close to family?"

"I feel like this question is fraught with peril," he teased.

"Why's that?"

"What if I tell you I do, and that with my sisters now come husbands and hordes of children?"

"I would say you're very lucky."

"Now, see, some women may find that to be a turnoff."

It was sure to be chaotic. Tara came from a large family, and their gatherings were crazy. But there was also something wonderful about it all, even if I hid in a corner most of the time. I loved seeing the shared affection and inside jokes. I especially loved the laughter of children. "For some, it might be a selling point."

He tilted his head. "Which category do you fall into?"

"I'll have to see how the night goes," I said in my best flirty voice, which may be questionable, but I was trying.

The way Seth's beautiful eyes lit up, it must have been a decent attempt. "I will do my best to be a great salesman, then."

I bit my lip, flattered he was already thinking he might want to see me again. Hope flared inside at the thought I might just be able to pull off scheduling love. It got doused real quick when . . .

"OMG, Natalie Archer, is that you?" Josh was using the girly-girl voice he had perfected in so many of his videos when making fun of women for everything from how much they loved Target to the obsession we had with having perfect eyebrows.

I clenched my fists and looked up to find the man I loved waltzing our way with the most devious grin of all time plastered on his face. I was going to strangle him.

Josh landed at our table, and Seth's eyes went wide and then kind of dreamy. "Josh Keller?"

"The one and only." Josh loved to be recognized.

"Man, I went to your show last year in New York with some old med-school buddies. We've never laughed so hard. That bit you did about how to write a country song was hilarious." He paused and pointed between Josh and me. "Wait. You two know each other?"

I was at least grateful he didn't seem to know we were acquainted or have knowledge of that video. Surely he would have connected those dots already.

"We go waaay back," Josh exaggerated. "We used to be like BFFs," he used his girly voice again.

"No way." Seth seemed astonished by the news.

I wanted to kick Josh. I couldn't believe he had shown up. That wasn't exactly true, but it floored me he actually would.

"Sorry to interrupt, but I just had to say hello to my old friend." Josh batted his eyes at me.

He was a dead man.

"You should join us," Seth offered.

My brow scrunched. What kind of guy invites another guy on his date?

Josh waved his hand around. "No. No. No. I couldn't."

"See you later—" I grumbled.

"Of course you can. I'm sure Natalie wouldn't mind." Seth didn't once look at me or try to get my take on the situation.

Because I certainly minded.

"Well, all right." Josh scooted his butt into my side of the table at light speed, pushing me farther into the booth, all while flashing me a charming smile.

I so badly wanted to elbow him in the side or dig a heel into his foot.

"I'm Seth, by the way." He held his hand out to Josh.

"Nice to meet you, man." Josh shook his hand while his other hand had the impudence to land on my knee. "It's really decent of you to let me crash your uh . . ."

"Date." Seth grinned at me before going right back to ogling my ex.

"Date?" Josh sang. "Wow, you're a lucky guy. This girl here is hard to get."

I pushed Josh's hand off the knee he was caressing, causing a flock of seagulls to take flight in my stomach. That was so not right.

Seth focused back on me, seemingly pleased I was hard to get. He had no idea. And the way this "date" was going, he had a snowball's chance in hell of ever getting the privilege of meeting me at another safe location of my choosing. "I can imagine she's broken a lot of hearts."

"You have no idea," Josh lamented.

I wasn't sure if I wanted to stab Josh with my fork for that comment or hug him. I pushed my fork farther away. I felt a bit stabby at that moment.

"How did you two become friends?" Seth asked.

It surprised me he hadn't considered the possibility Josh and I had dated. Most guys don't believe men and women can just be friends. Perhaps, though, he thought there was no way someone like Josh would ask me out. Or maybe he was just oblivious. Or it could be he was so starstruck, he couldn't think straight.

"It's a long story," I jumped in before Josh said something inappropriate or telling.

Seth smiled and shrugged as if he didn't really care for an answer to his question. "So, are you going on tour again soon?" He was back to fangirling over Josh.

Josh tugged on the collar of his T-shirt. "Probably. I have some things in the works," he didn't want to say.

I got his reluctance, but he didn't need to hide anything from me. I knew that was his life.

"Cool. I'll definitely get tickets."

Our server walked by, and Seth got his attention. "Can you bring my friend here a menu?"

I rolled my eyes and Josh laughed. I wasn't sure why. If he thought this helped his chances, he was in for a rude awakening.

Once Josh received a menu, Seth commented on his T-shirt. "I saw Aerosmith a few years ago in concert. What a ride. I dressed up as Steven Tyler for Halloween in high school."

"Dude, me too." Josh high-fived Seth.

From there, it was a mutual love-fest as they conversed about their adoration of seventies rock bands. The only good thing I could say about it all was that there was no need to feel self-conscious while eating, considering no one was paying attention to me.

The patrons in the restaurant were lucky enough to get serenaded as Josh and Seth sang a loud chorus of "Stairway to Heaven." And Seth did an air guitar solo of "In-A-Gadda-Da-Vida" even though the song came out in the late sixties. They both agreed it was a classic worthy of any decade.

I mostly sat in thought, contemplating whether I should even go on my date with Kyle this weekend. I knew one thing for sure: Josh wasn't going to know where we were meeting. In fact, I was kicking his butt out of my house for real this time.

"I just thought of this. It's open mic night down at the comedy club here in town. We should go. Man, how funny would it be if you got up?" Seth asked like a kid in a candy store.

Josh's face lit up at the prospect. It was exactly the kind of thing he would love to do. He turned toward me. "What do you think? Should we go?"

I placed my napkin on the table, more than done with the night. "I'm going to head home. I have to get up early, but you two have fun."

Seth's face turned a tad pink, and he cleared his throat. "I feel terrible. This wasn't much of a date, was it?"

"It's fine," I lied.

"Honestly, I feel awful. I'd love a rain check."

That wasn't going to happen. I gave him a placating smile before facing Josh. "Excuse me." He needed to get out of my way in more ways than one.

"Come with us, Nat," Josh pleaded.

There was one thing I was for sure never doing again, and that was going into another comedy club with him. I could see the pointing and hear the whispering now. No need to relive exactly how my life with Josh had been. I was completely overshadowed or silently mocked—in public, that was. There was no in between when I was with him.

"Goodbye, Josh." *Please let me go.*

fifteen

"Is it a love match?" Tara asked first thing when I called to tell her and Jolene about my disastrous date.

"I think Josh and Seth will announce their wedding any day now." I snuggled down into the covers, still not believing how the night had turned out.

"What?" Jolene roared.

"You heard me right. Josh showed up, and the two of them are a match made in heaven."

Tara giggled.

"It's not funny."

"Sorry," Tara snorted. "You're right, it's not. But it kind of is. The boy obviously has it bad for you."

That boy was an idiot. "He had the audacity to text me *I love you* on my way home as he headed to the comedy club with my date." Of course, I didn't check it until I got home. Safety first. I wished I would have never told him where I kept the spare key so I could lock him out. If only I knew how to change the locks. Maybe I could YouTube it. But did I really want to get out of bed and make a hardware store run late at night? It was tempting if it meant locking Josh out. Knowing him, he would call some locksmith and convince him this was his house, so it would all be futile.

They both went silent when I expected them to be outraged on my behalf.

"What?" I asked.

"Do you still love him?" Jolene asked.

"You know I do," I sighed. "But that doesn't mean we should be together."

"True," Tara agreed. "It's just that we've been talking, and it kind of says something that he's still staying with you. Are you, you know, friends with benefits over there?"

"Absolutely not. He's getting zero benefits."

They both laughed.

"What benefit are you getting from him being there?" Jolene got serious once she stopped laughing.

I curled into a ball, thinking about that hard but important question. "I don't know. He leaves his clothes everywhere, destroys my kitchen daily, and ruins my dates. Not to mention my schedule. So, I guess I'm getting tortured."

"You don't sound that upset about it," Tara commented.

"I don't? I mean, I totally am," I said half-heartedly.

"You can be honest with us," Jolene added.

I gripped the phone and let out a heavy breath. "Fine. I kind of love the torture. It's nice not to be alone. But I could get a puppy that would be just as destructive as Josh if I really wanted the company."

"The hair that dog would shed everywhere would drive you insane," Tara wisely said.

"This is true. But Josh leaves hair in my sink and tub," I complained.

"So, kick him out already," Jolene said.

"I'm going to. Tomorrow," I resoundingly responded, as well as I could anyway.

"Uh-huh," Tara sang.

"I'm serious. Tomorrow night at this time, he's going to be history. Caput. Put a nail in the coffin. Dead as a doornail. The end of—"

"You can stop with the idioms now," Tara interrupted me. "We get it."

I'm glad they got it. Someone needed to explain to me why Josh had to leave. I didn't mention it to my best friends, but I was still reeling from the *I love you* text. It's not like I didn't know he loved me, but he wasn't supposed to say it to me. Besides, I was back to abhorring him after he'd crashed my date and whisked away the Henry Cavill look-alike I had managed to halfway flirt with on our date. Actually, it was kind of the other way around. Seth was so taken in by Josh. In a way, it was creepy. But I'd seen it all before. The starstruck craze that came over almost everyone who met Josh, whether or not they knew he was famous.

"I should probably get to sleep. I'll call you tomorrow."

"Good luck," Jolene called out.

"Call us if you need us before then," Tara offered.

"I will. Good night." I hung up and stared at Lord Mac, who kept finding his way into my bed. "I guess it's just going to be you and me again. At least you don't leave the toilet seat up or steal my dates. If only you could kiss me until my toes curled. See you in the morning." I threw the covers over my head. I had a feeling it was going to be a long night with my thoughts. At the rate I was going, my thoughts and Lord Mac were all I would sleep with for the rest of my life.

I stopped and stared at Josh, who was dead to the world, stretched out on my couch in last night's clothes. I had just finished working out on my stair stepper. Sweat dripped off me as I watched him slumber peacefully. I had no idea what time he had gotten in last night or perhaps early this morning. All I knew was as soon as he was awake, he was out of here. I would cry about it later. I marched into the bathroom to shower, with thoughts of slamming the door behind me. The fool deserved an early wake-up call after his shenanigans last night. But I wanted to be well put together when I kicked his butt out. Don't ask me why, but I felt like I could be more intimidating dressed normally and not in a sports bra and shorts. Besides, I didn't want to give Josh the pleasure of seeing me with so little clothing on. He didn't deserve the honor. And maybe I was stalling. But only a little.

Once I was safely behind the door, I undressed and turned on the water. I continued to use Nana's frilly white shower curtain, which encircled the old claw-foot tub. I'd had the shower faucet installed not long after I'd moved in. I loved a good bath now and then, but showering was much more efficient. As soon as the water was a few degrees shy of the temperature of the sun, I jumped in, needing to relax my muscles. I blamed Josh for every knot in my back. Before I washed my hair or body, I let the hot water pour over me, breathing in and out deeply. Amid the mild ecstasy, I heard the door open.

I wrapped my arms around my chest. "Josh!"

"I just need to take a leak," he croaked in his morning voice.

"Have you ever heard of knocking?" I couldn't believe he had the gall to just walk right in. Scratch that. I totally believed it.

"I figured since you left the door unlocked, you wouldn't mind."

I wasn't used to having to lock the door, living alone for so long. "I totally mind. I'm naked in here."

"That was more incentive for me." He started relieving himself, to my chagrin. "Besides, if you're planning on getting married, you need to get used to this."

Oh. My. Gosh. "One. We are not married. Two. You have a lot of nerve waltzing in here. Especially after last night."

"It's not my fault we aren't married. And you should thank

me. Your doctor friend followed me into the restroom last night and the dude didn't wash his hands."

That news was so disgusting, I could hardly focus on how hurt Josh sounded when he said we weren't married. I would have to tell Stu to find a new doctor. How could the man not wash his hands after using the restroom? A public restroom, mind you. Could I report that to someone?

"Count yourself lucky I found out that tidbit for you."

I wasn't feeling all that lucky standing there covering my breasts while my ex relieved himself on the other side of the curtain.

Josh flushed and washed his hands. At least he had good hygiene.

"I can't believe you showed up last night," I tore into him. "How would you like if I would have interfered with your relationship with, let's say, Camila?"

He shut off the water. "You think you didn't? Hell, Nat, why do you think we broke up? You were everywhere, and I couldn't shake you, no matter how hard I tried."

I leaned my head against the wall, stunned by his admission. Even more, it pained me.

"I hurt her, Nat, because she knew I would never love her the way I love you."

A tear leaked down my cheek. Poor Camila. "I'm sorry, Josh. But don't you see how wrong we are for each other? Even last night, I didn't exist to you or to anyone. Your fans overshadowed me. Again."

"That's not what happened. I know how much you hate when attention is drawn to you, so I . . ." He paused.

He was right. I did my best to be invisible. But I hated it. It made me feel like a lonely child, begging for someone to notice me. "You ignored me. You and my supposed date," I finished his thought.

"No, I didn't," he said, more to himself than me, like he was having a hard time processing that it might be true. "All I thought about was you and how the idiot across from us didn't deserve you. What kind of guy invites another man on his date?"

I had wondered the same thing, which was why I would never go out with Seth again. "And then leaves with him," I added.

"Yeah," Josh whispered. "In my defense, I begged you to come with us."

"Why? So I could sit in the corner and watch how excited everyone would be when you showed up? Or worse, get recognized from the video of me going around? Is that what you wanted?"

"No. No," he spluttered. "I wanted you to be there so I could look into the audience and see the face I love the most in this world staring back at me."

Another tear escaped. "Those thirty seconds would have been lovely, but the rest of the night, I would have either been the woman who didn't exist or the 'why did he pick her over Camila' woman. Then we would have come home, and you would make me feel like I was the only person in the world in existence. And for a moment I would lie in your arms and believe you," my voice was choked. "But then reality would sink in, and I would remember I'm just your awkward girlfriend who was lucky enough to convince you we belong together. But deep down, we both know that's not true."

"The hell it isn't. You make it sound like you tricked me into loving you. How could you think that?"

"Look how different we are!" I begged him to see.

"So what? That's what makes us so great together."

"You say that because everyone loves you. You're the life of the party. I'm the cringey wallflower."

"You are the only one who sees yourself that way. If for just one second you could see how amazing you are, I wouldn't be standing here staring at your silhouette. Instead, I'd be joining you, doing my best to make you late for work."

I hugged myself tighter, longing not only for him to join me but for me to see myself as he did.

"And by the way, not everyone loves me, Nat. In LA, I'm not city enough. People tolerate me because I'm worth money to them. Worse, they kiss my butt, thinking they can get something from me. We all have our crosses to bear. I was hoping we could bear ours together. Let me help carry yours, and you can help carry mine." He took in a deep breath. "Don't you know how much I loved coming home to you? You were always my grounding force. But I only seem to hurt you." He sounded more defeated than I had ever heard him. "I'm sorry about last night. Just the thought of you being with another man kills me. I had to do something. But I realize now I'm the one killing you."

I slid down the wall until I was sitting in the tub, my knees to my chest, unable to hold back the steady tears rushing down my cheeks and mixing with the hot water. My heart was breaking because I knew he had finally seen the light. The horrible light casting the glaring truth—we aren't meant to be together.

"Natalie, I'm going to leave. But before I go, you need to listen to me. You can't schedule love. The best love comes out of nowhere. It's when you see a beautiful woman sitting in a corner, reading a book while a hundred people move about her, and she's trying her hardest not to be noticed. The best thing is, she doesn't even realize one can't help but notice her. Then something inside you commands you to do whatever it takes just for her to say something to you. And when she speaks, you know that's the voice you want to hear whispering good night to you every night in your bed. That's how love works." He opened the door, walked through it, and then slammed it.

My tears turned to racking sobs as I held on to myself, his words running through me like a speeding, out-of-control car. Each syllable crashing into my heart. At times, I did feel as if his life was killing me. But I loved him. So much. However, maybe this was the closure he needed. So, this was a good thing, right? Why, then, did I feel as if my world had just ended?

Sixteen

I LEANED AGAINST A WALL in the living room in my robe with wet hair. My heart continued to break as I watched Josh haphazardly throw his clothes into his trusted duffel bag that had seen better days. I resisted the urge to stop the madness and plead with him to let me properly fold and place them neatly into his bag. Under the circumstances, he probably wouldn't appreciate any packing tips. And if I spoke, I was afraid I would only beg him to stay. It was like staring at the door three years ago, wishing the knob would turn, but knowing it was for the best if it didn't. At least that's what I kept telling myself.

I was the girl who wanted to dance like no one was watching her but felt like everyone was watching me and it looked like a legion of bees was attacking me. Josh needed someone who was truly graceful in the public eye or didn't care she looked ridiculous while everyone watched. I was neither woman.

"You should sing more," Josh said out of the blue while shoving underwear into his bag.

I shook my head. "What?"

He looked my way and grabbed ahold of me with his red, watery eyes that said his heart was breaking as much as mine. "You should sing more. I heard you in the shower the last few days. You have a beautiful voice. Stop hiding it."

I think what he meant to say was, *"Stop hiding."* He knew

what he was asking. Only he was aware of my most embarrassing childhood memory.

I wasn't sure how to respond, but he didn't let me. He went right back to packing, if that's what you could call it.

"Are you going back to Tennessee?" I thought I should ask in case he had any trouble. I would know where to send help if need be. His old truck had a tendency to break down occasionally.

"Just long enough to catch a plane back to LA. I'm filming that damn pilot episode," he spat.

I would have thought he would be over the moon about it. "Congratulations. I know that's been your dream."

His head snapped up. "It's great. I get to trade one dream for the other," he barked. "I guess you can't have it all."

His not-so-subtle swipe made me wriggle where I stood, inside and out. "I'm sorry, Josh. I never wanted to hurt you."

"I know." He zipped up his bag with a vengeance. "I should have never come."

"Don't say that," I choked out, thinking it would have been for the best if he hadn't come. Except then I might not have found out about the doctor's handwashing habits until it was too late. I guess there was a silver lining.

"Why?" Josh pleaded to know.

"Because, as maddening as you are, I loved seeing you again. I love you."

He looked up at the ceiling. "The crazy part is, I know you do. Damn it, Nat. It wasn't supposed to end like this for us."

Against my better judgment, I ran to him and threw my arms around him for the last time, even though I knew it would do me in.

He didn't hesitate to wrap me up tight.

I nestled my head into his chest and sobbed while listening to the sound of his pounding heart. I soaked his shirt and breathed in his delectable scent, memorizing everything about him.

"I love you, Nat." Josh stroked my hair.

I tilted my chin up to catch his gaze already fixed on me—my lips.

Desire swirled in his gorgeous chocolate eyes. "Tell me you don't want me to kiss you and I won't," he whispered.

"Just because I want something doesn't mean I'm supposed to have it." Oh, but did I ever want his lips.

"Just because you're afraid of something doesn't mean you shouldn't have it." He leaned in. "Remember that," he said before his lips skimmed mine, testing the choppy waters we found ourselves on. When I didn't pull away, his lips pressed harder, gently moving over mine at first, taking his time until his hands found their way to my face via the long way. They had taken their liberties as they went roving over all my curves. I didn't mind. His touch enlivened me in a way nothing had in three years.

When his hands cupped my cheeks, his tongue unleashed its full power, prodding and tasting, until Josh groaned and my knees felt like they might buckle. Every feeling he had for me came crashing into my mouth. I felt the love, the anger, the hurt, his desire for more. The taste of the salt from both our tears mixed with it all.

I gripped his T-shirt, wishing for him to never let go but knowing we had to for both our sakes. As if he realized the same ugly truth, he abruptly pulled away.

We both took a deep breath in and out.

He stepped away, leaving me faltering. "The door is always open." In a fluid move, he grabbed his bag and sprinted out the door, but at the last second, he turned around. "By the way, I told the doctor I was in love with you and . . . he saw the video. Don't expect a phone call. I would say I'm sorry, but I'm not." He flew out the door, shutting it so hard, the house shook.

All I could do was stand there immobilized, not caring if the doctor ever called. Josh's words were assaulting my fragile heart. I wasn't sure which hurt worse: when he'd told me three years ago I could never come back, or this moment, knowing the door was open and all I had to do was find the strength to walk through it. I wasn't sure I could ever be that woman, as much as I wanted to be.

I lowered my shaky self onto the couch, sinking into it and wishing it could swallow me whole. Anything to take the pain away. Dang Josh for showing up just when I thought I had the perfect plan to find love. Part of me wanted to stick with the schedule just to prove him wrong, but the biggest part of me wanted to love myself enough to love him. The question was, how did I do that?

"Wow. We didn't think you would actually kick him out." Jolene sounded more than astonished over the phone when I told them Josh was gone.

"I didn't exactly kick him out. He left because . . . wait. You didn't think I could tell him to go?"

"Well, let's be honest, did you?" Tara asked.

"No," I whined, staring at Lord Mac, not wanting to work.

"If you didn't kick him out, then why did he leave?" Jolene was curious.

I relayed everything to them, even the doctor who didn't wash his hands in a public restroom. They were as grossed out by it as I was. I held back the kiss that infused my soul with all that was good in the world. "The real reason he left is because I don't love myself enough to be with him."

"Did he say that?" Tara asked.

"Not in so many words, but it's the truth."

"Nat," Tara started, "I don't think it's that you don't love yourself. I think you're just afraid to show it."

"What does that mean?"

"Like your therapist said, you've made too many good choices in your life not to love yourself. You just haven't been able to get over the fear factor."

"Fear factor?" I questioned.

"Yeah," Tara said. "You let your fear of pain control you."

In my defense, I had a painful past. It kind of does things to you. Not kind of—it wrecks you. In that wreckage, you learn how to lessen the pain, or you let it swallow you whole. "Alec has said as much to me." He also said on the other side of pain and discomfort is the reward. But the thing is, there is no guarantee you will actually get the reward. Hello, junior high talent show. Or let's go with more recent events, shall we? Bonjour, viral video.

"I just read somewhere that pain is inevitable, but suffering is a choice," Jolene jumped in.

I laid my head on the desk and moaned. "I'm suffering." I wasn't sure I had ever felt worse.

"What do you want to do about that?" Tara asked.

"I'm not sure. Josh is heading back to LA to film a pilot. He's on the verge of becoming a household name. And he mentioned something to Dr. I Don't Wash My Hands about an upcoming tour in the works. Also, I know I don't want to live in California. Did you know they have more damage-causing earthquakes than any other state? There are no warnings for those." At least with a hurricane you have plenty of warning it's coming for you.

"So, no Josh?" Jolene inquired.

I thought about the kiss Josh had just given me. There was something about the way he kissed that filled me like nothing else could. Did I really want to live my life without that? Without him? I thought I was okay to just love him from afar. Now I wasn't so sure. Why couldn't Josh be an accountant?

"I just don't know," I sighed. Alec's voice kept infiltrating my mind. "If Natalie could have her dream, what would it look like?" I hadn't thought about it because I knew exactly what it would look like. It would look like Sunday mornings snuggled up in bed with Josh, reading a book together until our kids jumped up on the bed. I could easily picture Josh grabbing the munchkins and tickling them until they giggled hysterically. Josh would, of course, want to stay in bed all day and let the kids eat in our room and get crumbs all over. I would be against it and insist we ate all meals at the table. We would probably argue about it in some cutesy voices since the children were present. I would, of course, win, and Josh would pout, but then we would make up that night and it would be perfect.

Somehow, in that dream, I would have an abundance of self-esteem and not care that Josh was famous. I would be like Matt Damon's wife, just a normal girl you don't hear a lot about unless you read one of those lists online about famous people who married non-famous people. We would live somewhere quaint, hopefully in Tennessee or South Carolina. Josh and I would agree to never spend more than a week apart. It could happen, right?

But what if that viral video of me never died and people constantly barraged Josh with questions about our intimate life and his psycho wife who scheduled everything? I got all clammy just thinking about it. It would be wonderful if I could just own it and not care what anyone thought. How amazing would it be if I could quip back, *"Don't you wish you were lucky enough to get an hour of sexy time every day?"* It did sound fantastic, but it was more like a pipe dream. Just like my girlhood dream of being on *American Idol*. We all know how my only public performance ended. If that was any sign of whether I could get over my stage fright or fear factor, whatever you wanted to call it, I would say the odds weren't good for Josh and me.

Seventeen

"THANKS FOR AGREEING TO SWITCH our date to today. This place is only open on Sundays now." Kyle smiled while opening the door to the Shoeless Joe Jackson Museum, which looked more like someone's residence. It had, in fact, been someone's house. At least that's what the website said when I'd looked it up. Joe Jackson, the famed baseball player, and his wife had built the place in the 1940s, but the foundation that had acquired it had moved the house several times. Of course, I'd had to do my research. I was pretty sure I knew everything I ever needed to about Joe Jackson, including that he'd only played shoeless once. I won't lie, that was kind of disappointing. Not sure why I expected him to have played in his socks every game. Regardless, I was giving myself props for changing my schedule around to accommodate Kyle's request. It honestly was a good thing, since I always took dinner to Hal and Stu on Sundays. It gave me the perfect excuse to end the date early if I needed to. However, Alec had still better give me another star on my chart tomorrow for being flexible. Even if I wasn't particularly excited to be on said date. But I had made a commitment, and it seemed very important to Hal and Stu that I give Kyle a chance. They were big fans.

I could see why they liked him. So far, he had been nothing but polite. You know, for the ten minutes we'd talked in the parking lot before walking in together. Kyle was handsome, with thick sandy hair, styled neatly. He had thoughtful brown eyes that unfortunately reminded me of Josh's. Although Josh's were a richer shade of brown and had the power to peer deep into my soul. Perhaps given time, Kyle's could do the same. Maybe if I didn't keep waiting for Josh to show up. Or wishing he would, though I had full knowledge that it was a selfish, unrealistic thought. If ever anyone had put the ball in my court, it was Josh. And there I was, staring at the ball lying lonely in the corner, too afraid to pick it up and take the winning shot. How many times had I tried to make a basket only to shoot an embarrassing air ball?

"You're welcome." I stepped inside the little museum. The smell of nostalgia, coupled with old books, lingered in the air. It wasn't bad. I liked that Kyle had thought outside the box. I love to learn new little pieces of trivia and history. And Hal and Stu assured me that even if my ex showed up, Kyle wouldn't ignore me or leave with him. Stu also informed me he was on the lookout for a new proctologist after hearing about the date and handwashing incident.

"Do you like baseball?" Kyle shoved his hands in the pockets of the well-fitting jeans accentuating his tall, athletic figure.

I bit my lip. "Honestly, I've only been to one game." I wouldn't mention it was a game I had attended with Josh. I had been on the road with him and we had a three-night stop in Chicago. Josh said it would be a crime if we didn't go to Wrigley Field while we were there. So, we caught a Cubs game. Admittedly, I knew nothing about the game. Josh had whispered the rules in my ear all night. That's not all he had said. No need for details, but I remember finding a new appreciation for baseball that evening, despite the crowds of people. Whose existence was drowned out by Josh's whisperings.

"But I enjoyed it," I added when Kyle was crestfallen over my lack of baseball enthusiasm. I didn't elaborate on my enjoyment. I really needed to figure out a way to not think about my ex on every date. Assuming I went on any more. Hal and Stu had some more men lined up. I think they quite enjoyed playing matchmaker. But Josh had me shook. I was torn between living in fear and tackling those same fears like a three-hundred-pound linebacker. A little fear isn't a bad thing. It keeps you safe. And in my case, possibly lonely. Unless Kyle was magical and could help me forget all about Josh. Like Karen Carpenter would say, "We've only just begun." Who knew what the next few hours had in store?

"I'm glad." Kyle shifted his feet like he was nervous. It was kind of adorable. "I played in high school and college."

"That's great. Did you want to go pro?"

"Nah. I didn't want to be on the road half the year, living out of a suitcase."

I perked up. Huh. Maybe there were some possibilities here. "Believe me, I'm on the same page. Did you know that people who travel frequently for work are more prone to depression and anxiety?" I blurted, before thinking about what I was really saying. Showing him I'm a weirdo who looks up odd facts like that daily. But I supposed it was better for him to know that up front. Visions of him running out the door began flooding my mind.

But then ... he grinned a huge grin. "They're also more likely to smoke and become dependent on alcohol."

He had no idea what a turn-on that statement was to me. Could I have possibly found my weirdo? Suddenly, the yellow walls of the museum got brighter. Kyle's face lit up as well, like he had the same thought about me.

"Can I introduce you to one of my heroes?" He beamed with pride.

I assumed he meant Joe Jackson, considering his boyish excitement in the parking lot just moments ago.

"I would love that."

"Fantastic," he said, relieved. "Right this way." He led us to some encased White Sox jerseys.

I followed him. We were seemingly the only patrons.

A sweet gray-haired man who ran the place shuffled our way. "Welcome, welcome," he croaked. "Let me know if you have any questions."

"Thank you," Kyle politely responded. "If you don't mind, I would like to lead the tour today," he teased.

"Be my guest," the old man responded before painstakingly going back the way he'd come.

Kyle bounced on the balls of his feet eagerly.

I appreciated his enthusiasm.

"Do you know the story of Joe Jackson?" Kyle asked.

"Uh . . . well . . . I read up on him, when you said this was where we were going," I admitted. "I like to be prepared." I wrung my hands together.

He tilted his head, a serene, almost dreamy look in his eyes. "What a thoughtful thing to do." So he didn't think that was odd?

This was good bordering on excellent.

"Some people might call that bizarre. Maybe even controlling."

He shrugged. "Who needs those people?"

Right? Who needed go-with-the-flow extroverts who threw caution to the wind at every turn? Obviously, I needed Tara and Jolene. They totally understood me. We shall not mention the other extrovert who also got me. He required possibly more than I was capable of—to love myself so wholly that we could spend eternity together arguing over which way the silverware was supposed to go in the dishwasher—fork and knife handles up, and spoon handles down. That was when he cared to do the dishes at all. Not thinking about it.

"I like the way you think," I replied.

"I'm glad." He smiled. "I guess you don't need my spiel about Joe since you've done your research."

"I'd love your take on him. The World Series scandal is fascinating." It was said Joe Jackson and his team, the White Sox, intentionally threw the 1919 World Series. Officials permanently banned him and several of his teammates from baseball because of the allegations.

"Are you sure? I can go on and on about it. I actually wrote a paper about it, vindicating Joe."

"Really?" Sounded like something I might do.

"Yeah." He seemed embarrassed. A quality I liked.

"Let's hear it, then. Make me a believer." I realized the double meaning of what I was asking. I needed to know if I could find love outside of Josh. Not that I needed to know if Kyle and I would fall in love—just that the possibility existed.

"Okay. Just remember you asked for it."

I nodded.

We moved closer to the old jerseys.

Kyle grabbed his phone out of his pocket. "Let me pull up Joe's stats during the series. Numbers don't lie."

Numbers may not lie, but stats could. It was all about how you manipulated them. I kept that to myself. I was sure as an actuary he knew that. Besides, I didn't want to be controversial on our first date.

Kyle scrolled his phone, and I couldn't help but notice several pictures of a raven-haired beauty kept popping up. He was in many of them with her. They were a nice-looking couple. I wondered if she was his ex-fiancée. I wasn't judging him for having so many photos of her readily on display. Hello, I was just making out with my ex a few days ago. It was a kiss I couldn't get off my mind. For someone who loved to control everything, and prided herself on doing so, I was having a difficult time mastering my thoughts of late.

"Here we go," Kyle said, helping me to focus on something besides the way it felt to be in Josh's arms. "See here." Kyle pointed at a bunch of numbers that meant very little to me. "He had twelve hits, three doubles, a home run, and six RBIs." He might as well have been speaking Greek to me, except I would have understood at least some of those words. Thank you,

Duolingo. "I mean, come on," Kyle was indignant on behalf of his hero. "Does that sound like a man who was throwing the game?"

I shook my head and smiled, not sure what else I could do. I was trying to figure out what *RBI* stood for. I would google it later.

Kyle scrolled through more data, spouting out more useless info to me. Not that I minded. I was glad to see he was passionate. It caused me to wonder if he was one of those men who watched sports 24/7. I should probably find out. I didn't want to be with someone who incessantly watched TV.

"Do you watch a lot of sports?"

He looked up from his phone. "Only when the Braves are playing. Other than that, I find it to be mostly a waste of valuable time."

I liked that answer.

"How about you?" he asked.

"No." I laughed. "I usually allow myself an hour of TV a day."

"Impressive. What do you do with your spare time?"

"Right now, I'm learning French, and I love to read."

"Est-ce que tu parles français?" he asked with perfect diction.

"Très peu," I responded, pleased he knew French, or at least enough to ask if I spoke it. The answer was very little. Not enough to run away to Paris yet.

"You understand it, though."

"I'm trying."

While we moved into the next room, he asked, "What else are you interested in?"

"Art and serial killer documentaries," I said without thinking.

"Me too," he admitted.

Okay. This was getting too good to be true.

"Really?"

"I find them fascinating." He stared at some old baseball cards encased in glass.

Part of me liked his answer, but the paranoid part wondered if he found them interesting because he was taking notes on how to become one. I stepped away from him despite the thorough background check I had run. Ever hear of the BTK Killer? The man was a psycho who killed ten people all while having a family of his own, going to church, and being a "normal" member of society.

"Why is that?" I tried to ask in a non-accusatory tone.

"Actually," he shifted, "my fiancée, I mean, ex-fiancée, is a forensic psychologist. She acts as a criminal profiler for the Philadelphia Police Department."

"That has to be an incredibly hard job."

"It is . . . but she's amazing at it," he hesitated to say.

"Did you live in Philadelphia before moving back to Greer?"

He rubbed the back of his neck. "Just outside of it."

"Did you like it there?"

He let out a heavy breath. "Not really." He pointed to the cards in the case. "Do you know how much one of Joe Jackson's cards went for a few years ago?"

I wasn't sure why he would ask me that. Maybe he thought I had run across it in my studies. I shrugged, waiting for him to give me the price tag.

He paused for an unnaturally long time. "I shouldn't have complained like I did."

I tilted my head. "Complained about what?"

He startled, coming out of his thoughts. "Sorry, I . . . uh . . . I was just thinking that I probably didn't give Philly a fair shot."

I wasn't sure what to say, so I went with a generic "Oh."

He waved his hand around. "It's neither here nor there. It's ancient history." We moved on to the next room.

"How much did the card go for?" Now that he had posed the question, I needed the answer.

"Uh . . . almost half a million." He sounded distracted.

"Wow. That's a lot of money for a card with a guy's picture on it."

"It's history," he responded casually.

Well, I'll take my history in a book. It's much cheaper.

"You know, there are a lot of great historical sites in Pennsylvania," he said offhandedly.

Anyone who took American history would know that. "Did you visit any of them while you lived there?" I had always wanted to go see the Liberty Bell and the Betsy Ross house.

"Several. Mindy," he said her name reverently, "was a history buff."

No doubt Mindy was the ex-fiancée.

"Anyway." He led us into the kitchen.

I thought I had a small kitchen, but this one took the cake. It surprised me how modest the home was, given Joe Jackson's fame. Maybe I shouldn't have been so surprised. My ex was quite famous and made a lot of money, but to look at him, you wouldn't know. He drove an old truck, his clothes were nothing to write home about, and he never lived anywhere fancy.

I pointed at the counter. "Those are cute cherry canisters."

"Mindy loved cherries," he sighed.

I saw where this was going—nowhere. I should have known it was too good to be true. It was my luck to find a man who had a boring, stable job, knew French, wasn't obsessed with TV, dressed well, smelled good, etc. and was more than obviously still hung up on his ex. Again, no judgment. I was right there with him.

"Do you want to talk about her?" I offered. Might as well. There was no way I would get involved with a man who was still in love with another woman. Oh. Ouch. That gave me some pause. Like a major stop. How could I expect a man to fall in love with me when my heart still belonged to Josh? I suppose I hoped someone had the superpower to steal it back and claim it as his own.

Love Rescheduled

"No. No. No. I'm so sorry. I'm embarrassed."
"Don't be. I get it. Tell me about Mindy."

Eighteen

"Let me get this straight." Alec could barely hide his grin. "You spent the entire date talking about his ex, and then you encouraged him to call her. Are you feeling okay?"

The truth was, I wasn't feeling all that great. I was feeling pretty hopeless about the scheduling love situation. Listening to Kyle cry over Mindy while we sipped lattes had put a big damper on it. She sounded like an incredible woman. She solved cold cases and worked with troubled youth. Her only "defect" was that she loved Philadelphia, a place she had poured her heart and soul into, trying to make it a safer place one solved crime at a time. That and she couldn't stand baseball, but Kyle found that endearing.

Kyle hated the traffic and, oddly enough, the crime. Not like anyone liked crime, but there were levels. He wanted a quiet life . . . He also wanted the person he loved more than anything. It was all too familiar.

"I'm fine," I lied. "He obviously regrets leaving, and it's not like she's famous or humiliated him in a viral sort of way. And he's a pretty self-assured guy with a normal, loving upbringing, as far as I can tell. Besides, I don't know if they'll work out their differences. But he needs closure."

"Huh." Alec grinned. "And how do you know this?" He was totally baiting me.

Was I going to swallow the hook? Yep. I grabbed on to that big, juicy worm. I'd had two of the worst dates ever in the last week, and the man I loved left me. I needed Alec to reel me in and help me in a big way. "Because," my voice cracked, "I know how it feels to be so in love with someone but fear a life with him would make you both miserable."

Alec gave me a sympathetic look. "I take it you're not doing well with Josh leaving?"

I scrunched my nose. "Wait a minute. How do you know Josh left?" I hadn't mentioned that yet. I saved that fun for later. As well as the unsanitary doctor story, which involved Josh.

Alec cleared his throat. "I just assumed," he stuttered.

"Oh, no. Don't give me that. You talked to him, didn't you?"

"You know I'm not at liberty to say."

"But you were obviously talking about me."

"You frequently mention the presumed client."

"Just say his name." I got touchy.

"Natalie, I shouldn't have said anything."

It was too late now. "What did he say?"

Alec pretended to zip his lips. "I'm not saying a word."

"Fine." I pouted.

"So, how do you feel about him leaving?"

"You're not my therapist," I reminded him, though I most certainly treated him like one, but that wasn't the point.

"True, but as this has a direct correlation to your goals and personal growth, I believe it's an appropriate question."

"How do you think I feel?" I snapped back.

"Judging by your tone, I would say not well."

"I'm sorry for snapping at you, but I can't believe you're talking to him. You were mine first." I sounded like an insolent child.

Alec grinned. "I'm glad you love me so much you don't want to share," he teased. "But you're not answering the question. Why is that?"

I took a deep breath in and sank into my chair at the table. "Alec, he wants the seemingly impossible."

"Which is?"

"He wants me to be someone I'm not."

"Explain," he prompted.

"You know, love myself unconditionally, blah, blah, blah, not care about what anyone thinks about me, yadda, yadda, yadda. The usual."

"Sounds terrible," he deadpanned.

"It is," I whined.

"What are the obstacles holding you back? Or do you even want a relationship with whatever his name is?" Alec chuckled.

I gave him a small smile in return for his attempt at humor. Yet, I thought about his questions. The obvious answer to the first question was me. It was always me holding me back. The answer to the second question was a little more complicated. Yes, I wanted a relationship with Josh, but making that happen scared me more than anything ever had. Because ... "Let's pretend I get out of my own way, and we try to work things out. And say it all goes great for a while, just like it did before. But then ... it gets hard again. I can't keep up the act and Josh realizes he doesn't really want someone as boring as me. Then what?"

Alec's brow furrowed. "First, I thought we were working on speaking kinder to ourselves."

I said nothing. I was failing miserably at that assignment.

Alec continued, "Are you basing your decisions on hypotheticals?"

"No. There is a track record here," I defended myself.

"Do you mean of you trying to control the outcome before allowing it to play out?"

"Uh ..." I fell back against my chair. "No," I stammered, my heart beating uncontrollably, knowing I might possibly be lying to myself. The jury was still out.

"Natalie," Alec spoke in his *I'm about ready to explode some truth bombs on you* voice. "You need to be honest with yourself. You are so used to—"

My phone started violently buzzing next to my laptop. I only kept it out to mark the time of our session—one hour exactly. I tried to ignore it, but then I noticed the name popping up in the notifications—Zac. He was in my contacts, but I had forgotten. It was more surprising that he had kept my number. My pulse raced. The only reason he might contact me was to tell me something was wrong with Josh.

"Alec, I'm sorry, but I have to check my phone. Josh's best friend is texting me." My voice shook unnaturally.

"Really?" He rubbed his chest, not sounding all that surprised.

I held my breath and swiped the phone off the table. Facial recognition immediately opened it. I clicked on the texting app, eyes squinting, fearing the worst.

Zac: *I told you to stay away from Josh. You're ruining everything.*

"You're ruining everything," I repeated out loud, looking at Alec, who was swallowing hard. "What does he mean?" I said, more to myself. Zac was happy to answer in the next text.

Zac: *You're not worth him throwing away what could be his one big shot.*

I dropped the phone, sick to my stomach. There were several more messages in the same vein. Each one made me feel like the girl on the junior high school stage who had lost everything that day, including the only shred of courage she ever had. Josh surely could not be thinking about walking away from the pilot he was supposed to be filming. My worst fear could come to fruition. What if Josh walked away and he discovered I wasn't worth it, just as Zac suggested? He would always resent me, just like my parents did for being born.

"What's wrong?" Alec leaned in and asked.

"Josh," I eked out. "He's . . . he's . . . he's making a mistake."

"That's not your call now, is it?" Alec challenged me.

"You knew about this?"

"Knew about what?" he feigned any knowledge.

"Alec, please tell me he isn't giving up his dream for me," I pleaded.

"Natalie," he said tenderly, "you can't control Josh or his dreams."

I pushed my chair back. "I may not be able to control him, but I will talk him out of this insanity."

Alec let out a heavy sigh. "You're looking at this all wrong."

"No, I'm not," I cried. "Don't you see if he does this, he's going to end up hating me? He can't hate me." I broke down, tears streaming down my cheeks.

"Is that what this is all about? You think you've been preventing him from hating you?"

"That's been my hope." I grabbed my phone and dialed Josh's number.

Alec sat and watched wide eyed, not saying a word, but his facial expression screamed to put the phone down.

Josh's phone rang and rang until it went to his voice mail that instructed, "Hang up and text me." He hated talking on the phone, unless he was on the road and it was me. Even then, he preferred a video call. That had likely changed. Surely it had. If not, he would hate me soon enough.

"Josh, please call me," I begged. "Zac just texted me. I won't let you give up your dreams, do you hear me? You've worked too hard for this. Please, don't do this." I hung up and stared at the phone.

"Natalie," Alec said, carefully. "Have you ever stopped to consider the only way he will come to hate you is if you keep your distance from him?"

I slowly looked up from my phone. "I wish that were true. Excuse me—I have to go."

Alec shook his head. "I don't think you're looking at this in a healthy light. Where are you going? Our hour isn't up yet."

I had this feeling Josh wasn't going to call me back. He could be more stubborn than me. He was going to leave me no choice. "I'm going to LA."

Alec's jaw dropped.

"I know. I don't make spur-of-the-moment decisions, but I have to talk him out of this."

Alec grinned the biggest of all grins as if he knew something I didn't. "I think that's an excellent idea. Good luck."

I was going to need more than luck. I was going to need a mild sedative, a bottle of hand sanitizer, throw in some sanitizing wipes for good measure, and a slide deck presentation to make my case. Believe me, I would need something to do on the plane so I didn't hyperventilate. This was so not on my schedule.

Nineteen

"YOU'RE DOING WHAT?" JOLENE YELLED through my car speaker.

"You heard me right; I'm going to LA." I had to keep saying it, as I hardly believed it.

"Are you talking on the phone in your car?" Tara asked, astonished.

I had a no-talking-on-the-phone-in-the-car rule, even if it was hands-free. I had never once used my car's phone capabilities, but . . . "Desperate times call for desperate measures." My plane left in under an hour, and I was trying not to have a panic attack as I raced to the airport—going the speed limit, of course. I hadn't gone completely rogue. It was bad enough I wasn't getting to the airport two hours early. Which was usually a waste of time, considering how small the airport was in Greenville. Although it did boast of its status as an international airport. But that was neither here nor there at the moment.

"Yes, I'm using the hands-free car option. If I die in LA, I've left you both the cottage and Lord Mac, assuming he doesn't die a spectacular death with me. Be gentle with him. He likes to sleep on a pillow."

They both giggled.

"I'm serious."

"That's the funny part," Tara sniggered. "You're not going to die in LA. Lord Mac will be safe and sound."

Love Rescheduled

"I don't know. Josh better not make me have to take an Uber or rent a car. He'll come get me at the airport, right?" I could hardly breathe thinking about the unsavory possibilities. I'd left Josh several messages, telling him I was coming. No response yet. I kept wondering if he already hated me. Or if this was a trick to see if I really would come to LA and he was just making me sweat it out. I was sweaty all right. I'd done some major hustling trying to pack a proper bag and make online reservations, all while maintaining my commitment to this insane plan. It was a major workout.

"I'm sure he will," Jolene didn't sound very convincing.

"Maybe I shouldn't go," I wavered. Except I had just spent more on a nonrefundable airplane ticket than I ever had. I was sick over it and would eat rice and beans for the next month. This is what happens when you do things unscheduled—mass chaos. Hence, after this minor episode, I would be in full-blown schedule mode, trying to detox from this erratic behavior. One day Josh would thank me. When I was watching him on TV, it would all be worth it. As long as he didn't make me take an Uber.

"I think this is exactly what you need to do," Tara said.

"You do?"

"You need a little shakeup in your life. It's good for the soul. And admittedly, I think Josh is good for you, too."

"We aren't getting back together."

Jolene snort laughed. "Right."

"I'm serious. I only packed a bag for one night. I'll show him the slide deck I'm making on the plane to convince him how wrong he is, and that's that. I'm coming back home late tomorrow."

"Jolene, what are the odds Josh doesn't play sexy and dirty and convince her to stay a while longer?" Tara asked.

"Survey says, odds are not in Nat's favor," Jolene replied.

"You ladies are hilarious," I said flatly. "Listen, this is a business only trip."

"Ooh, business," Tara sang.

I stopped at a red light, almost at the airport. "Not that kind of business."

"Uh-huh." Jolene wasn't convinced.

"I mean it. I just don't want him to hate me," I whimpered.

"Nat," Tara spoke gently, "I don't think it's possible for him to hate you. If he was going to hate you, he'd already feel that way."

"That's not true. He's never given up his dream before. He'll regret it and then resent me. I can't let that happen."

"I'm not sure that's your call." Jolene basically repeated Alec's admonishment.

"I know." Truly, I knew I couldn't control his actions, but I was going to do my best to convince him otherwise.

"Good luck, honey," Tara called out. "Call us when you land."

The light turned green, and I proceeded into unknown territory. "Thank you. I will. Oh, and will someone please check the seismic activity in LA and then text me? I didn't have time before I left."

They broke out into fits of uncontrollable laughter.

"You're going to be fine," Jolene assured me.

That was yet to be determined.

As soon as I found a parking spot in a garage across from the airport's terminal, I hopped out of the car with my bag and called Josh one more time. "It's me again. Please pick up or text me back. I don't know if this is some game of chicken for you, but I swear I'm coming. I texted my itinerary to you. Don't make me call Zac and ask for your address. I'm not sure he would even give it to me. He said some hideous things about me earlier. I'll probably need to revisit my therapist because of it. Maybe he's right; maybe I have played with your heart and emotions. You have to believe me: it wasn't intentional. Josh, I love you. I've only ever wanted what's best for you. I'm not worth passing on what you've worked your entire career to achieve. That said, please, please don't make me have to call a stranger for a ride. I don't know if, after all of this spontaneity, I can handle it."

I hung up, even more unsure if I should get on the plane. What if Josh didn't come? What if he didn't want me there? But... what if this was my only chance to talk him out of ruining his career? Did I love him enough to sacrifice my temporary emotional well-being to save him? I'd loved him enough to leave him, even though it had broken my heart. So, the answer was yes. For Josh, I would do this one last thing. Then I would walk out of his life forever. And not be the "ho bag" Zac had accused me of being earlier.

I clicked my key fob to open the back hatch and grabbed my carry-on, hoping my best friends took mercy on me and texted me a seismic report. The likelihood was low. Maybe if I hustled, I could check before the plane boarded.

I rushed through the parking lot and took the elevator to the lower level. I swore a couple of women recognized me on the way down and whispered conspiratorially. It was enough to make my skin crawl and think of going right back up and forgetting this entire thing. It was also a good reminder of why Josh and I weren't compatible.

When the elevator door opened, I hesitated to get off, but then I thought of a world where Josh hated me. That I couldn't have. I mustered up all my courage and marched off the elevator, the cold humidity sweeping through the garage and seeping through my jacket. It was more incentive to cross the street and get to the terminal, if only to be warm. I stood waiting to cross the busy road where people were dropping off and picking up passengers, dreading getting on the plane. Being out in public drained so much energy. It's hard for introverts to *people* all day, especially when they can't go home at night and rest in their little cocoons.

As soon as it was safe, the waiting group was being herded across the road. Halfway to the other side, I swore I heard Josh call my name. Wow. I was apparently having hallucinations. No doubt brought on by my irrational behavior.

"Natalie," I heard Josh's voice yell again.

This time I looked around, praying I wasn't going insane. That's when I saw Josh's head bobbing in the crowd walking toward the parking garage as he tried to push his way through.

I stopped in the middle of the road, sure I was having some sort of mental breakdown. Why would Josh be here? I was flying to LA to see him.

The surrounding people didn't appreciate me holding them up, judging by the dirty looks they threw my way as they maneuvered around me. But I couldn't move as I watched Josh run my way, carrying his old duffel bag. It was like being in a dream montage in a movie. It was so surreal; I couldn't trust it.

"Natalie," he said, out of breath as he neared.

"Josh," I could hardly speak, fearing this was a delusion. "What are you doing here?"

"I came to see you. Where are you going?" He stared at my luggage, crestfallen.

"Didn't you get my messages? I'm coming to see you."

"I turned my phone off before I boarded the plane at the crack of dawn this morning. I haven't turned it back on. All I wanted to do was get to you. I was picking up my rental car."

I couldn't help but smile at the foolish man who was obviously a glutton for punishment coming back here.

"Wait . . . You're flying to LA? Now?" He seemed confused. He wasn't the only person befuddled at the turn of events.

"Well, that was the plan."

"Why, Nat?" He seemed not only surprised but pleased by the thought.

I grabbed his hand and pulled him back to the sidewalk closest to the parking garage.

His tight grip spoke of never wanting to let me go. That was going to be a problem.

A few people kept stealing glances at us, recognizing Josh.

The fishbowl feeling was back in full force, and so was my upset stomach. I pulled Josh into the parking garage, hoping to gain some vestige of privacy.

Not even a second after we found refuge near a concrete barrier, Josh discarded his bag and took me into his arms, his lips landing on mine.

"Josh," I mumbled against his impatient lips.

"I don't give a damn who's watching. I need you, Nat." His mouth covered mine, begging me to let him consume me. I dropped my defenses, along with my suitcase, and let him envelop me. I didn't know if that made me weak or if it was a show of strength on my part. But I needed him as much as he needed me in that moment.

When I didn't hesitate, he pulled me closer and deepened his urgent kiss, groaning as he pressed his body against mine. He tasted like the Biscoff cookies flight attendants hand out on planes. It was the best taste in the world. While his tongue explored my mouth, his hands intertwined with my own. For a moment, I forgot why I was flying to LA. All I wanted to do was stay in our little world, wrapped up in each other.

"Natalie," he said, like he revered my name above all, as he took a breath and then tugged on my lower lip with his teeth. "I love you. Please don't push me away."

A sudden rush reminded me why I was flying to LA. "Josh, you shouldn't be here. You're making a mistake. Zac texted me."

"That slimy bastard. I told him to stay out of it before I kicked his butt out last night."

I'd never heard him talk about his best friend like that. "You kicked him out? Why?"

"Let's talk about it later." His lips went in for another round.

Regrettably, I pressed against his chest. I wanted nothing more than to kiss him again, but he was more important. "Josh, we can't do this. You need to go home. Film your pilot. Please," I pleaded.

He placed his hand over mine and held it against the

Fleetwood Mac shirt covering his chest. "I am home when I'm with you."

I looked up at the concrete ceiling, tears welling in my eyes. "I can't have you resenting me. Worse, hating me. Josh, I'm not worth this."

"The hell you aren't. That's your parents talking."

I lowered my gaze, only to be struck by his blazing eyes. "It won't work between us. Please quit making this harder than it already is."

"You're wrong. And I was wrong to leave last week. Hell, to let you go three years ago. That's what you know in your life because your idiotic parents taught you that's what you do when it gets hard. But I'm going to show you that you're worth fighting for. That we're worth the fight—that we're worth all the fights."

He had no idea how much I loved the sound of that, even ached for it, but . . . "You can't magically fix me."

"You don't need to be fixed. You need to be loved."

I leaned into him, resting my head on his chest, realizing that all I really wanted in life was to be loved just for me. My parents had never given me that, and so I never thought I was worthy of such love. Any hint of trouble in relationships just solidified it. But maybe it wasn't true. Maybe it didn't spell the end. "Did Alec tell you that?"

"No," Josh chuckled. "But he helped me to realize some other things."

"Like what?"

He exhaled loudly. "I'm not happy in LA," he admitted.

"You're not?"

"Not at all."

I clung tighter to him. "So, what are you going to do?"

He leaned away, a mischievous glint in his eyes. "For starters, I'm going to prove to you I'm not going anywhere. After that, I don't care, as long as we're together."

"Josh, you say that now but—"

He silenced me with a soft kiss on my lips.

I closed my eyes and reveled in his gentle touch.

"Nat," he whispered. "Stop telling me how I feel. I know what I want."

"I want to be with you too." Especially considering my last two dates. If that was the pool I had to choose from, I had no desire to dip my toes into it. Or maybe my problem was that I had never jumped out of the waters of Josh. I still had a problem, though . . . "But I don't know how to have you."

"I guess it's a good thing I'm an excellent teacher."

"Is that so?"

"Yes, ma'am. And your first lesson starts right now."

"And what's that?"

"First, I have to say . . . Damn, girl, it's so hot that you were going to fly to LA. That has to tell you something."

I knew what it said to me. It said I loved him more than anything. "What does it say to you?"

"You want me *so* bad."

I rolled my eyes, but he wasn't wrong.

"You know I'm right." He was so full of himself.

"Perhaps," I played coy. "So, what is this lesson you want to teach me?"

"I figure you have a lot of unscheduled time on your hands since you won't be able to make your flight now." He wagged his brows. "I think it's time for you to learn the fine art of spending the day in my arms while I whisper in your ear all the things I love about you."

"That can't take very long."

"That's where you're mistaken. I think we might need all night, too."

"Josh—"

"Shh." He placed a finger on my lips. "Before you tell me why it doesn't fit into your schedule—"

I removed his finger. "I was just going to say I can't wait to hear what you have to say." My only hope was that I could learn to believe him. And . . . that I didn't let my schedule get in the way.

twenty

I RAN A FINGER OVER Josh's stubbled jawline, outlining his handsome face while I lay in his arms, snuggled up on the couch. We hadn't talked much unless you counted nonverbal communication, which, let it be noted, was unscheduled. "I still can't believe you're here. Thank you for not making me get on that plane. I will be forever grateful." I smiled. I wasn't even that bothered by the money because of how thankful I was I didn't have to be on a crowded, germ-filled flight to the land of earthquakes and ridiculous traffic.

Josh nuzzled my nose with his. "I can't believe you actually decided on a whim—in the middle of the day, no less—to fly to LA."

"Me either. All I kept thinking about was how I couldn't allow you to hate me."

"I've hated you once, and it didn't work out so well."

Ouch. Those words stole my breath. "You hated me?"

"I don't know why that surprises you. When you left me, you took the thing I loved most in life, and I hated you for it. Nat, I was going to ask you to marry me. I'd already bought the ring, but I was waiting to pop the question since Nana had just passed away."

I swallowed down my guilt and my heart. So many emotions

and memories from that time filling my chest, making me feel uncomfortable. "I know."

His eyes widened, a hint of fury in them. "You knew?"

"I wasn't exactly sure, but I had a feeling. And I knew if you asked, I couldn't say no, so I left." I remembered how he kept hinting about the type of ring I might want. He had talked more about our future. It scared me because I was afraid he wanted something I couldn't give him, in the end leaving us both miserable.

"Why would you do that?" he sounded as broken as my heart felt having to admit that truth to him.

I leaned my forehead against his, breathing in the scent of his Obsession for Men, reminding me he was here. "Because I knew you wanted to move to LA, and big things were happening for you. I didn't want to hold you back because I wasn't ready for any of it."

"Natalie, I would have stayed in Nashville; you know that."

"I knew that. That's why I left. You deserved your chance."

"You're maddening," he growled before skimming my lips with his own. "But I guess I handed you further confirmation you were right since I let you go with hardly a fight. I was just so hurt you would leave, knowing how I felt about you. My pride got in the way."

"I know I hurt you and I'm sorry. But I couldn't see how it could work out, and honestly, I still don't. Josh, I can't let you give up your dreams for me."

He took my face in his hands. "When I landed in LA last week and got off that plane, I thought, what the hell am I doing? I don't even like living here. The script for the pilot is awful."

"It is?"

"So bad."

"Then why were you doing it?"

"Because a bunch of people who don't really care about me kept pushing me to do it to benefit themselves, including Zac," he growled his name. "But here you are, just as you've always been, thinking about what makes me happy, never using me. So let me tell you what makes me happy. It's easy. It's you."

"Josh," I sighed. "You don't know how much I love to hear that, but . . . you know it's not that simple. You can't just walk away from your career. You know in the end it won't make you happy."

"You don't know that. I could be a proctologist like that idiot Seth. Although my patients probably wouldn't appreciate the jokes I would tell in the examination room concerning their 'problems.'" Josh laughed, making me laugh too.

"I don't see you going to med school for years on end."

"That's probably a good call. What was the last yahoo's profession you just went out with? Actuary? I could look into that. By the way, how did your date go?" he hesitated to ask.

"Kyle is a nice man who is still very much in love with his ex." That was all that needed to be said.

Josh grinned a should-be-illegal grin. "So, you had something in common."

"You could say that."

"Let me say some other things, too." His thumbs caressed my cheeks. "I love you, Nat. We will work this out because all I know is my career pales in comparison to you."

"This can't be a one-sided thing. You shouldn't have to give up anything for me."

"Why? You were willing to face death for me today."

"Death?" I questioned.

He chuckled. "I remember all your stats about earthquakes."

I was not in the least bit ashamed of it. I had made a slide deck about the state of California the moment Josh mentioned moving there about four years ago. "Living on a fault line is only asking for trouble."

"Yet you were still coming to *save* me."

"Well, that's because I love you, and I thought you were being irrational and idiotic. You still might be, by the way."

"I'm going to enjoy every second of it," he groaned before pressing his lips to mine.

I closed my eyes and focused on the shivers his tongue produced as it slid across my lips and tickled my mouth. And how his leg twined around mine, making me feel as if we were one. I loved when his hands moved down my body to interlock our fingers together. It was as if he were saying, *Hold on tight while I make you my world.* It always amazed me how softly his lips could move over mine, yet still send electric shocks deep down to my toes. That was, until I was on the brink of pure ecstasy and I basically attacked him, ever deepening the kiss and entangling our limbs, just as I did at that very moment. He loved it and fully took part until we were both out of breath.

When the fires of passion cooled and the kisses simmered into gentle virgin kisses, as Josh called them, I rested my head on his chest, listening to the hammering beat of his heart. "We need to make a plan on how to make this work."

Josh's fingers danced down my arm. "How did I know you were going to say that?"

"Because I'm predictable, but I'm also right. There has to be some balance. Like you can't become a doctor. That won't make either of us happy."

"What will make you happy?"

"This isn't bad, for starters." I snuggled closer to him.

"Noted. What else, Nat? What can I do to prove you are enough for me?"

"I don't know. I've never felt like I was enough for anyone. And let's be honest, I made you miserable when we were together."

"False. All of that is false. I've only been miserable away from you."

"But we fought all the time about our time apart, or worse: our time together on the road."

"That's because we were looking at it all wrong."

I lifted my head off his chest. "How?"

"I was talking to Alec—"

"I can't believe you stole my Alec."

Josh guffawed. "Come on, honey, we can share him."

"Perhaps," I teased. I was curious about what Alec had to say.

"As I was saying, Alec thinks all this time we've been taking a zero-sum approach. We thought for either of us to get what we wanted, one of us was going to have to miss out. Instead, we should have been more willing to compromise."

"Compromise how?"

"Like . . ." He swallowed hard. "What if I buy Laugh on Tap and only tour one month of the year and . . . we both move back to Nashville?"

I blinked an inordinate number of times. "Is that an option? Is Mikey selling the place?"

"He's been thinking about it, but he wants it to go to the right person. He's hoping that person is me."

"But what about your big-screen dreams?"

"Nat, for the last three years I've been chasing that dream, and it's felt nothing but meaningless. Every time I came home to Zac, I questioned what I was doing with my life."

I narrowed my eyes. "You looked so happy on social media."

"I had to keep up appearances for my brand, but I haven't been happy for a long time. About three years, to be exact, until I saw you at the club."

"Where you humiliated me."

"You're not going to let that one go, are you?"

"People are still talking about me," I complained.

He cringed abashedly. "I really am sorry. I swear on my life, I will never use you in a routine again. And I won't ask security to detain you if you try to run away from me. Next time, I'll jump off the stage and tackle you myself," he joked.

"Funny," I fake grumbled.

"Honestly, though, what do you think of moving and running a business with me? One where I can be home every night to tuck you in and say dirty things to you." He nuzzled my neck, tickling me with his scruff.

I twisted my hands in his T-shirt, giggling but thinking most seriously about what he was offering. And admittedly, about the dirty things he loved to say. "That's huge. I don't know what to think. It's kind of hard to think of leaving Greer." It had been my cocoon. A hideaway, even.

Josh met my eyes. "That's valid. What is it you like about living here?"

It impressed me he didn't argue with me; instead, he validated me. He must have gotten that advice from Alec. "It's small, but not too small. And there's Nana's cottage and Stu and Hal. And . . . well . . . it's easy to hide here."

Josh gazed at me while mulling it over. "What if we moved outside of Nashville, near my parents? Franklin's pretty cozy. We could keep the cottage and rent it out. And you could visit Stu and Hal. We could even fly them to Tennessee."

"Uh . . . that's a lot to think about." I started hyperventilating a bit. There was a possibility I would need a bag. Not that I wasn't amenable to thinking about Josh's proposition, but my well-ordered, schedule-loving self could only take so much in one day. "And are you really sure you want to run a business? What about your videos and big tours?" I managed to breathe out.

"Shhh. Calm down." Josh stroked my hair and kissed my forehead. "I know I threw a lot at you. We don't have to decide tonight; I just wanted you to know I'm willing to compromise. Hell, I'll even promise to put my dirty underwear in the hamper every day and put the fork and knife handles up in the dishwasher." He smirked.

"Uh-huh. We both know that will last for all of a week."

He tapped my nose. "You're probably right. But I am serious about being home every night. Nat, the last three years have made me realize that all the fame in the world means nothing when I have no one to share it with. As long as I can make people laugh, I don't care where I do it. If I run the comedy club, people can come to me."

I wasn't sure what to say. I needed to process it all. But he gave me some hope. Alec was right: I had to stop thinking about this as a zero-sum game. We just had to figure out the right compromise that didn't stifle his dreams or crush me in the process. That was possible, right?

"I know what you're thinking, and I promise we can work it out." Josh answered my unspoken thoughts. "But we don't need to tonight. Just let me hold you."

I could do that. Except . . . "I need to stretch and wash my face."

Josh shook his head playfully. "Or, maybe you could be a tad flexible," he carefully suggested, "and just this once, not leave my arms."

"You want me to compromise?"

"Yes, if you can manage that."

I thought for a moment. Rationally, I knew it wouldn't be the end of the world if I didn't wash my face or stretch. No one was going to judge me for it, least of all Josh. I had to think about what was most important. I gazed into Josh's eyes. In their reflection, I saw myself. They told me what he held most dear. I could do the same for him. After all, I would still be on a plane right now if it weren't for him. There was no way I would have stretched in front of so many people. But Josh was my people, and I wanted to keep him that way. So, I pecked his lips and snuggled in next to him, mentally giving myself a star on my chart for breaking routine.

Josh immediately relaxed and held me as close as he could. "I love you."

"I love you too."

For several moments, we said nothing, only breathed in and out, our thoughts floating between us in the semi-dark. One thought wouldn't leave my mind. "Josh," I whispered into the silence. "What did you do with the ring you bought for me?" I asked, hoping I wasn't pouring salt into his wounds. The pure loathing on his face when I walked away from him three years ago made much more sense now. I had stolen more than I knew. Yes, I'd had my suspicions, but I didn't think he had bought a ring.

"Are you still hoping to keep your wedding date?" he responded lightheartedly.

"I do pride myself on keeping my schedule, but I wondered if perhaps you gave it to—"

"I would never do that to you or Camila," he said firmly.

"I'm sorry. I wasn't accusing you."

"Don't apologize. I shouldn't have snapped at you. It's just that she found the ring in my sock drawer."

"Oh."

"She asked me to get rid of it, and I told her I couldn't. We both knew then it would never work between us. Honestly, I think we knew from the start it was a bad idea. Regardless, I hurt her, and I'm not proud of that."

I stilled in his arms, feeling awful for all the terrible things I had ever thought about Camila. Well, mostly. She had gotten cozy with Josh, and I would have to scrub those images out of my head. However, I was sorry for the pain my memory had caused her. I was well acquainted with gut-wrenching rejection, and I didn't wish it on anyone. Not even women who were intimately acquainted with the man I love. "She must hate me."

"She doesn't," Josh was quick to say. "She encouraged me to come after you."

"Really?" She was a better person than me.

"Camila knows we're good together, and she's happy with her husband."

"I'm glad." Truly I was.

Josh's hand glided down my back. "I still have the ring." His heart started hammering even harder.

My heart was in a race with his to see whose could pulse faster. "You do?"

"It's yours whenever you want it. Just say the word and we'll keep that date of yours."

OH. WOW. It almost seemed too good to be true. I could save the date *and* marry the man I love. Maybe it was time to start believing in my dreams. Could I schedule that?

twenty-One

"HAL AND STU, THIS IS JOSH."

Both men folded their arms as they sat on their regular bench and eyed Josh warily. As much as they appreciated a man going after what he wanted, they were still salty about the humiliation of it all. So was I, but every time Josh kissed me or spoke a reason why he loved me in my ear, I found it harder and harder to stay mad at him. Besides, the man was willing to become a proctologist for me. If that didn't spell true love, I wasn't sure what did. All joking aside, we had a lot of things to iron out. I knew there would be some heavy compromising going on. We were meeting with Alec tonight in a joint session in the hope that he could help us reach a mutually beneficial conclusion.

"Nice to meet you." Josh held out his hand, not at all deterred. Odds were in his favor—they would be best friends by the time my walk was over. It was his superpower. Josh was compromising and following my schedule today. In return, I promised him extra time on the couch tonight. I might even get crazy and delay washing my face until morning again.

I told Josh he needed Hal and Stu's approval before we could proceed, as well as a business plan. Josh said he knew I would say that and was already working on one. He'd even hired a consulting firm to assist. He impressed me.

"So, this is the fella who embarrassed you." Hal refused Josh's hand.

"Yep." I smiled.

Josh flashed me a *thanks for that* grin. "I'm actually the fella who loves and adores her." He held his hand out farther.

Stu scrubbed a hand over his double chin. "That remains to be seen."

"You better have a sit-down with us while Hepburn here walks," Hal directed.

"We have some other men lined up for her." Stu winked at me.

I wasn't sure Hal and Stu were the best matchmakers, but I played along. "Great. You can give me their info when I get back."

Josh dropped his hand, throwing me an incredulous look.

I playfully shrugged. "What? A girl has to keep her options open. September thirtieth will be here before I know it."

Josh leaned in and kissed me. "I can't wait to see you walking down that aisle toward me."

That thought brought warmth to an otherwise brisk day. "Well," I squeaked, "I will leave you gentlemen alone. Have fun." I waved.

My old men had a lot of questions in their eyes. I supposed I would have to explain the whole scheduling-my-wedding-date thing to them. Or maybe Josh would.

Josh grabbed my hand and pulled me in for one more kiss before I walked off. Normally, I wasn't one for PDA, but in front of Hal and Stu I didn't mind. If only I could feel that way around everyone. It reminded me of Alec's parting words yesterday before I rushed to the airport:

"If you keep letting people's perceptions about you rule your life, you will never be the person you are capable of being. You will never have what you want until you let go of others' opinions." It was a real doozy. I hadn't had much time to think about it in all the weirdness that was yesterday. Here I thought I would present a slide deck and then cry all the way back to Greer. Instead, I'd spent the night on the couch with Josh while he enumerated all the reasons he loves me, including my schedule-loving ways. Apparently, it was a real turn-on for him. He'd said he needed someone who was better at managing time than him. Tara was right: Josh wanted a yin to his yang.

Of course, he was hoping I could be a little more flexible. I was going to try my hardest. Honestly, I wasn't even opposed to moving back to Tennessee, which reminded me I better call my best friends. I knew they were dying for an update after the brief text I'd sent in the car as Josh drove us home from the airport yesterday. After he'd sworn he wouldn't tailgate or drive like he was a NASCAR star.

I grabbed my phone out of my pocket and dialed Tara while making my way around the park. Look at me going off the schedule and calling them while I was on my walk instead of after.

Tara picked up right away. "Spill your guts, but wait just a second. Jolene," she shouted, "get in here. Nat's on the phone."

I held the phone away from my head and rubbed my ear. I think she might have popped my eardrum.

"We have been dying over here," Tara informed me. "It is so freaking romantic. He was flying to see you, and you were flying to him, and then y'all met up at the airport. Please, let me use this in a book."

"Sure."

"Thank you. But tell me, was it more of a Hallmark or Lifetime scene at the airport?" That was how she judged steaminess levels. Hallmark being sweet and Lifetime on the spicier side.

"Well . . . um . . . he pushed me against a concrete barrier in the parking lot." I was still hoping no one saw that.

"OMG. Totally Lifetime. I'm so proud of you. Look at you getting all sexy in public."

"I wouldn't exactly categorize it that way."

Tara laughed. "Please let me live vicariously through you."

"I take it the professor still hasn't called." She had been agonizing over it the last few days. It had been a week since their last communication.

"I should probably be thankful for it. He's so broody. Unfortunately, I find it to be attractive."

I could understand that. There was something appealing about the Mr. Darcys of the world.

"I'm here," Jolene stated. "Tell us everything."

I looked behind me at Josh sitting between Hal and Stu. He already had them laughing. Although it made me happy, I rolled my eyes. I loved that quality about Josh. "I'm not sure where to begin. To sum it up, he wants to get married and for us to move back to Nashville." I didn't mention buying Laugh on Tap, as that was to remain confidential between Josh and Mikey for now.

"Shut the front door!" Jolene yelled.

"Do it," Tara demanded. "We miss you."

"I miss you guys, too. But you know it's not that simple. We have some things to work out. Well, mostly, I feel like I need to figure out how to be a part of his life and not feel invisible or like I'm going to lose my mind."

"So what are you going to do about that?" Jolene challenged me.

I stopped walking, noting her tone that said, *It's about time you truly take* control *of your life*. A random thought popped into my head that all the things I'd tried to control were only keeping me from truly owning my life. Perhaps it wasn't such a random thought as it was the truth. Was Alec right? Could letting go of others' opinions actually give me the control I longed for? It would give me what I wanted most in my life—love. Love for myself and the love of my life—Josh.

"I'm going to do whatever it takes."

The cold air whipped my cheeks as I sailed through the air on the swings. I hadn't swung in forever and never on the swings in this park, though I walked by them almost every day. How sad was that? I had missed out on something I loved because they didn't fit into my schedule. Josh convinced me to try them out after he charmed my favorite old men. He was good at that—helping me remember there is more to life than work and schedules. I should enjoy it, too. He exemplified that and other things as well. He was already best friends with Hal and Stu. They had planned a poker night for the next day. Josh was in charge of the chips and dip. He also got the guys to agree he should be the next man I went on a date with. Maybe my old men would make good matchmakers after all.

Josh pushed me, helping me to go higher. "I love watching you swing. You look so carefree."

I closed my eyes and swung my legs, feeling lighter than I had in a long time. "Don't get used to it," I teased. But really. He shouldn't. I knew I had a lot of self-work to do, but I never saw myself becoming totally carefree.

Josh chuckled and grabbed the swing on the way back, holding me in place. Really cradling me as if that's all he ever wanted to do. He took a moment to peer into my eyes. Such adoration shone from his own. "I still can't believe we get another shot. I know you're still mad at me for the club scene. Honestly, I don't care if you stay mad about it forever. I'm just glad it happened. When I saw you that night, everything changed. I knew I had to do whatever it took to have you back in my life . . . because you are my life."

It was kind of hard to stay upset with someone when they spoke to you like that. Especially when they meant every word.

"I guess everything did change that night, didn't it? I know more still needs to change. Please be patient with me."

"Nat, I don't want you to change. I just want you to be happy. I hope that includes being with me."

"Me too." I leaned in and kissed him.

"Mmm. I like that. Very much." He let me go and pushed me until I was sailing again.

I hated to ruin the moment, but I needed to talk to Josh about something important. "Jolene mentioned Zac is spreading rumors about you and making a jerk of himself on social media. Did you know that?"

"Yep." Josh didn't sound too concerned.

I stopped swinging so I could properly gauge his reaction. I would freak out if it were me. It had been me, and I was still flipping out about it. "You don't care?"

Josh shrugged. "What can I do about it?"

"But he's your best friend."

Josh scoffed. "Not anymore. At some point, I became a meal ticket to him. He doesn't care about me."

"I'm so sorry. But aren't you worried he might damage your reputation?"

"Nah. I make fun of women all the time in my videos, and guess who makes up most of my live shows? Women. The idiot can say what he wants about me. Those people out there"—he pointed off in the distance—"they don't know me, and they don't really care about me, so why should I care what they think?"

I could think of a dozen reasons but went with, "It could impact your brand. Or what if he says bad things about me?"

Josh came and stood between my legs. Thankfully, it was chilly enough that there weren't any kids on the playground. I was sure their parents wouldn't appreciate the overt affection. He rested a cold hand on my cheek. "Nat, I know how much you worry about what people think of you. I hate that your parents didn't tell their little girl she was enough and worthy to be loved."

Tears began pouring down my cheeks. My therapist had often talked about that little girl. How I needed to heal her before I could see life through a different lens. I was more than impressed Josh knew that, too. Maybe he could help me, as I hadn't been successful yet, or he could at least hold my hand through the process.

"Let me tell that girl now it wasn't her fault her parents couldn't love her." He brushed a few tears away with his thumb. "She was more than enough, and you are too. Neither of you needs to give a damn what anyone thinks." He grinned. "Whatever Zac may spout off will say more about him than it does about us. But—" He paused. "If he says one word about you, I will rain down hell on him," Josh seethed.

I looked up at Josh and thought, *Why in the world did I ever walk away from him?* The girl inside me answered. *Because I was afraid.*

I think it's time to let go of that fear. What do you think?

I was a victim, but you don't need to be. Don't let our parents win.

My inner self was pretty smart. I didn't want to be ruled by anyone anymore, especially my parents. They didn't deserve to have that power. The little girl inside me deserved so much more.

"Josh, I know you don't believe love can be scheduled. But how do you feel about *rescheduling* love?"

He gripped the swing chains and leaned in closer. "Hmm. Rescheduling love? That could work. Assuming you're talking about us."

"Definitely us . . . Always us."

twenty-two

"How's it going?" Alec asked with a big, toothy grin.

I curled my feet under me as I sat on the cozy couch in the afternoon light filling Josh's parents' sunroom. Josh had returned to Nashville a few weeks ago, so I was visiting him while he attempted to hash out the purchase of Laugh on Tap. He was in serious negotiations with Mikey and his team of lawyers. Josh had lawyered up, too. What a whirlwind several weeks it had been. I have to admit: it surprised me how business savvy Josh is. He'd graduated with a degree in business well over a decade ago, but he'd always called it a throwaway degree because he never intended to use it.

"I feel like when you ask me that now, you already know the answer." Josh talked to him more than I did. Not only was Alec doing relationship coaching with the both of us, but he was helping Josh identify what was most important for him career-wise and personally. Personally, I was at the top of his list.

"Girl, you know that you're still my favorite. Don't tell any of my other clients that."

"Your secret is safe with me." I smiled.

"But really, how are you?"

I thought back through the last six weeks, starting with New Year's Day, when I'd discovered I had scheduled my wedding. How crazy it seemed. Even crazier now that I might very well keep that September date. Josh was all for it. He was just waiting for me to say the word. In my heart, I knew I would eventually ask for the ring. The ring I had thought about so often. What did it look like? Where did he keep it? How much pain had it caused Josh to carry it around with him all these years? I asked him why he'd kept it, and he said because the ring belonged to me and he wasn't willing to let go of anything he equated with me. When he said things like that, I wanted to rush headlong into our future.

With both Josh's and Alec's encouragement, I had gone back to therapy. This time with a therapist specializing in childhood trauma. Dr. Stone was helping me heal that little girl inside me. She was helping me understand I needed to give validation to that girl and acknowledge her as a victim, but it didn't mean I had to be one. It was kind of odd for me at first, but Dr. Stone was teaching me how to be the mother the girl inside me never had but desperately needed. It was weird to talk to myself in such a manner. To say things to myself like, *"You matter. You're safe. I will support and protect you."* These affirmations helped me talk adult me down when I began worrying what others might think about me or even say about me. It made it easier now to stop and think what I as a mother would say to my own child. It was amazing how much that perspective had helped me. Not to say I was anywhere close to perfect at it, but at least it gave me enough courage to be with the man I love.

"I'm doing well. I'm mostly enjoying the course you recommended from your friend." It was a ten-day workshop on how to train your brain to stop destructive thought patterns.

Alec chuckled. "It's uncomfortable for you, I take it?"

"You could say that, but only because it's hard to let go. Why is it so difficult to let go of things we know are bad for us?"

"Because it means letting go of part of yourself. I think we fear what might replace those pieces we slough off. But here's a hint: your best-self fills in the gap."

"That's the hope."

"I think you're doing a great job. What do you want to be coached on today?"

I sat back and smiled. "I don't even know where to begin. There's so much going on. Josh and I are trying to strike a good balance between my rigid schedule and his laissez-faire approach and a long-distance relationship." I'd told Josh I wouldn't move back to Nashville unless we were married. That seemed like a good compromise, especially since we had spent so much time apart the last few years. We weren't exactly thrilled with the physical distance between us now, but it wasn't like last time. Somehow, I think we innately knew we were going to last. This wasn't a zero-sum game, so the physical separation was more bearable.

"How's that going?"

I turned my head from side to side. "We haven't killed each other yet." I smiled, thinking of our daily battle of wills when we were together. Let's just say there was a lot of making up on those nights, which almost led me to believe Josh was purposely being stubborn. He was an evil genius.

Alec barked out a laugh. "When it comes to compromising, what are your goals?"

"I'm hoping to avoid jail time," I joked.

Alec rolled his eyes.

"Okay. Honestly, it's getting better, especially since Josh has more work things to focus on. And when we are together, I shift my work to the hours between eight and five because Josh believes we should leave evenings open for spontaneous fun on the nights he isn't performing."

"Yes, how did you feel attending his show last night?" Last week, Alec had helped me visualize attending and not feeling uncomfortable or like an outsider. He helped me to see I am worthy to be there as Josh's girlfriend.

I thought back to the night before at Laugh on Tap. Jolene

and Josh had both performed. I'd sat right up front, which I never had before. I was used to watching him from backstage. But I'd learned that Josh had always wished he could look out into the crowd and see me. I knew Jolene felt the same way. I was finally starting to believe these wonderful people truly love me and want me in their lives. Watching their shows from the crowd was the least I could do to show them how much they mean to me.

However, Tara had to hold my hand through it all, literally and figuratively. There was still a lot of buzz going around about Josh and me. Including his fallout with Zac and the stupid joke he'd told about how I scheduled everything. Quite a few times last night I had to close my eyes and calm the little girl in me. It was worth it as Jolene and Josh brought down the house. There was a sweet moment at the end before Josh exited the stage where he'd pointed at me and mouthed, "I love you." I'd gone so far as to attend the after-party. I read a book in the corner . . . but this time it was from Josh's lap. It was all about the give and take. Josh had me by his side, and I didn't have to *people* all that much.

"I'm not going to lie," I responded to Alec. "It wasn't easy, but I walked away from it mostly unscathed. Maybe even a little proud of myself." Especially when Josh had me pose in a picture with him for some fans. Totally not my thing, but I was grateful it was me he wanted to put his arms around and not anyone else.

"Girl, you are getting a star on your chart."

I bowed. "Thank you."

"What can we do to help keep you moving forward on this path to a healthier, happier you?"

I contemplated that question. "We should probably keep the relationship sessions going. Do you think you could help Josh visualize wiping the sink after he uses it?"

"I'm sure I can help him visualize it, but whether he does it is another story," he quipped.

"Ugh," I groaned. Toothpaste and saliva in the sink made my stomach roil a bit. "If Josh and I ever buy a house together, we are getting separate bathrooms." Though I had a feeling he would still use mine.

"Great solution," Alec complimented me. "Speaking of which, how are we feeling about getting married?" He cleared his throat.

At first I bit my lip, but then it dawned on me. "You're being Josh's spy."

"What, girl? No," he stumbled on his words.

"You're totally lying. Doesn't this go against some honor code for coaches?"

Tomorrow was Valentine's Day, and I kept wondering what Josh had in store. He had been tight-lipped about it but adamant he wasn't giving me the ring until I told him I wanted it. It's not that I didn't want it. I was just cautious.

I knew one thing we were doing, and that was my podcast with Tara and Jolene. It was a special Valentine's Day edition. My best friends had begged me to let Josh be part of it, knowing full well what that was going to do for the show's popularity. I had agreed but warned them we still weren't going to use my name or photo. But Alec was making me wonder if Josh had more in store. Was Josh going to propose? There was no question I would say yes. Did it scare me? Absolutely. Was I going to make a slide deck about how to properly clean a bathroom for his reference? Definitely. I was sure his response would be to hire professional cleaners. We were going to drive each other crazy for eternity. I looked forward to it. I'd done life without Josh, and I wasn't willing to again.

"Girl, you know I would never play you like that." His smile said differently.

"Uh-huh."

He laughed.

Laney, Josh's mom, walked in. "Oh, I'm sorry. Am I interrupting something?"

"Hey, Mrs. K.," Alec called out.

"Oh, Alec." Laney came in and sat next to me. She was the

cutest woman. Petite and delicate, with long dyed-blonde hair. And she always smelled like sugar cookies. In fact, I think she was baking some now for Valentine's Day. "I was just telling Josh we need to invite you for Easter."

Of course Laney was already friends with Alec. I believe Josh inherited his superpower from his mom. She and Josh's dad, Kent, certainly made me feel very welcome. Very much like a daughter.

Case in point. Laney took my hand in her own, holding it like a mother would, or more like should.

I inched closer to her. There was something about her that made me feel safe.

She squeezed my hand.

"I would love to visit," Alec responded.

I had never once thought about meeting Alec in person. What a shame. I needed to be better about things like that.

"Marvelous," Laney exclaimed. "I better let you two get back to business."

"That's okay." I smirked at Alec, denying him the ability to pass any information on to Josh. "I think we're done for today."

"Girl, I love you, but that's cold. All off the record," Alec teased. "I'm still charging you for the full hour." That he was serious about.

"I would expect no less. Goodbye." I waved before clicking out of my screen.

"I hope I didn't make you cut your session short," Laney worried.

"Not at all," I assured her, more curious than ever about what Josh had planned for tomorrow.

Her eyes lit up. "Good. I was hoping we could have a little girl time before Josh and Kent get home."

It was moments like this where I had to ask myself what was most important to my well-being. Keeping to my schedule or loving the people around me? I was ahead of schedule with the book I was editing. And I was finding the more I allowed people in and stopped trying to control every aspect of my life, the happier I became. Who knew? Don't get me wrong: I would make up the missed work somehow. That was just how I rolled. But I was discovering life didn't always need to be a series of items on a checklist. My therapist was helping me see I was using those things to hide from the pain. Now I was trying to work through it despite the pain the journey had caused.

"What did you have in mind?"

"I thought we could decorate some cookies and watch a rom-com," she said excitedly.

I had to swallow down my emotions. It's something Nana would have suggested. More than that, it was something I always wished my mother would have done with me. I carefully glanced at Laney. It hit me that she came with the Josh package. Could I be so lucky to get the man I love and a mom? "I'd love that."

"You just made my day." She let go of my hand to stand, but then she reached right back out for me. It was a simple gesture, but she had no idea how much it meant to me. Laney, Josh, and Kent kept reaching out for me even though, once upon a time, I had done my best to push them away.

I anxiously gave her my hand, hoping she would know it was my way of saying thank you. She could have easily hated me for breaking her son's heart; instead, she saw my own hurts and loved me despite it all. That was a real mom.

She led us to her huge cavern of a kitchen with fancy appliances, rustic wood cupboards, and gorgeous stone countertops that were covered in dozens of cooling heart-shaped cookies. There was a built-in desk with a good-sized TV on it. I remembered watching many football games on it during dinner, to Laney's irritation. She believed mealtime was sacred family time. Her husband and son believed otherwise when Tennessee was playing.

"Do you mind if we watch *An Affair to Remember*? I love the old classics and Kent hates them," she bemoaned.

"Not at all. I love Cary Grant. My nana used to say, 'When

God created Cary Grant, he patted himself on the back for a job well done.'"

"Nana sounds like my kind of gal." She winked. "Have a seat." She waved to the stools around the large island.

I wished Nana and Laney had met. There was no doubt they would have been the best of friends. I took a seat while she turned on the movie and brought over some cookies along with piping bags of royal icing in shades of white, pink, and red.

The dramatic music of the old film played. There was something so comforting about sitting next to Laney and enjoying the movie together.

"Now, darlin', don't worry if you mess up. We'll just eat that one." She nudged me with her shoulder.

"I think we'll eat a lot of these." I wasn't artistic in the least bit.

She held up a bag of pink icing as if she were toasting me. "Music to my ears."

I grabbed a cookie and some red icing while we watched Deborah Kerr put Cary Grant in his place. Those darn celebrity men. I could totally relate.

"I'm so happy you and Josh are back together," Laney said offhandedly while masterfully filling in her cookie with the shimmering icing.

"Me too."

"I had a feeling you would find your way back to each other."

I tilted my head. "You did?"

She nodded. "You were too good together. But I think Josh had some growing up to do first."

I raised a brow. "Josh?" I thought for sure she would have blamed it all on me.

"Don't sound so surprised. I love my son, but he has his faults, like everyone."

"He is a slob," I pointed out.

"I know," she said, exasperated. "He gets that from his

father. He can also be singularly focused and miss the bigger picture."

I set down the piping bag. "What do you mean?"

She placed her perfectly iced cookie on a tray. "Kent and I told him a long time ago that LA was not where dreams come true. But he had to figure that one out on his own."

I shifted on my stool. "I worry that someday he might regret not doing that pilot."

"Oh, honey, don't you see how content he is? Sometimes you have to travel down the wrong road to know which one is right."

Didn't I know it.

"Josh," she sighed. "I knew he wasn't happy in LA. He tried to cover it up, make jokes about it, but I knew." She rested a cheek on my hand. "You opened his eyes to see the road home, and I'm not talking about Nashville." She pointed at my heart. "This is where he belongs. Careers and opportunities come and go, but none of it matters unless your heart is in the right place."

I let her words settle in my soul. I, for one, knew my heart was finally at home.

twenty-three

"REMEMBER, YOU CAN'T USE MY name, and no sexy comments to give away who I am," I warned Josh in his truck before we walked into Tara and Jolene's condo to do our live podcast.

Josh snorted. "Anyone who knows Tara and Jolene knows it's you."

"True, but most of our listeners don't." And I knew after tonight we would have a lot more. Josh was sure to post about it on his social media platforms.

"Fine, but my hands will have some fun under the table." He wagged his brows.

I unbuckled my seat belt and slid across his bench seat. "You. Are. Incorrigible."

"Guilty," he groaned, leaning in to kiss me. His lips hovered over mine, begging me to come the rest of the way.

"Happy Valentine's Day," I whispered before my lips landed on his.

"Very happy," he mumbled before deepening the kiss, making me wish we could get straight to our date. I couldn't wait to give him my gift—Aerosmith tickets and a custom-made nameplate for his new desk at Laugh on Tap. Mikey and Josh had signed a tentative agreement yesterday. If all went well, in ninety days Josh would be the proud owner of Laugh on Tap. He had big plans, including some renovations and bringing in more big names, including his own.

Josh's hands tenderly enveloped my face. "Nat, I love you," he spoke between breaths.

"I believe you."

He leaned away. The contentment his mom spoke of was written across his cute face. "I think that right there is the best gift you could give me tonight. Well . . . almost."

"What else did you have in mind?" I asked, coyly.

"You'll see." His lips brushed across mine.

"Maybe if you give me a hint, you won't be disappointed," I tried to coax it out of him. I'd been trying to get him to tell me all day what we were doing to celebrate. I wasn't exactly a huge fan of surprises. All he would tell me was that it didn't require me to dress up and I should probably wear some comfortable shoes and bring a coat. The coat part didn't thrill me. I didn't love the cold. But I loved him, so I would see where the night took us.

He nipped my lower lip. "I'm not worried."

"Fine," I pouted.

Josh laughed. "I promise you will look back on this night and think, *Josh is a genius.*"

"We'll see." I pecked his cheek. "We better get in there." I grabbed the cookies Laney and I made, as well as the flowers I'd purchased for the very best friends a girl could ask for. I knew this would be an especially tough night for Tara, as the professor seemed to have ghosted her. And I was trying to be better at showing them exactly what they meant to me.

Josh opened the door and helped me out of the driver's side, grabbing the cookies for me. His warm hand engulfed mine, and we hustled to the condo. Spring couldn't come soon enough. I missed warm nights.

Jolene and Tara opened their door before we could even knock. They were both wearing devious grins. Were they plotting with Josh?

I gave them each a scrutinizing glare as we handed them their gifts and walked into what they called "the estrogen zone." They seemed genuinely pleased I had thought of them. I smiled at their new furniture, which included furry blush Himalayan chairs and a velvet couch covered in unfolded laundry. I refrained from going over and folding their clothes, though it made me twitchy to not remedy the situation.

Tara noticed my agitated state while she grabbed a vase for the pink roses. "Don't worry, the laundry will get folded just how you taught us."

"I could help." I headed in that direction, pulling Josh along with me.

"Step away from the laundry," Jolene commanded in her best police officer voice.

"But . . ." I cringed.

Josh tugged me toward the kitchen table where the mics had been set up. "Breathe, Nat, breathe."

"Have her face the wall," Tara suggested through her snickering.

"If we just fold the clothes now—"

Josh silenced me with a kiss. "We will waste valuable time."

I slowly breathed in his scent and focused on the dimples I adored so much, reminding myself it was okay if my best friends wanted to live unruly lives. "Okay." I let out a long, slow breath.

"You get another star on the chart," Josh teased me.

I sat in my chair, facing the wall, trying not to focus on how there were some unsightly holes where they had taken down photos of their exes over the years. Actually, I think darts had made some of the marks. I could picture them tossing sharp objects at the professor's head. In my attempt to ignore the holes, I put my headphones on and turned on the mic. It was nice to be doing this in person with my best friends. I typically phoned in.

Josh sat next to me, and as soon as his headset was on, his hand rested on my thigh and began caressing it.

I did my best to pretend he wasn't causing shivers to course through my body while simultaneously creating an urge to cancel the podcast and skip to whatever else Josh had in mind. Hopefully someplace quiet where we could be alone.

Josh's impish grin said he knew he was getting to me.

Well, two could play his game. My hand danced across his thigh until he grabbed it, holding it in place.

I smirked at him, knowing I had beat him at his own game.

Tara and Jolene eyed us from across the table.

Jolene flipped a few switches. "It's cute and all that you're in love, but don't make us hate you. Especially since the only good night kiss I'll be getting tonight is from Fred." Fred was her tabby cat.

Tara puckered her lips. "I'll kiss you."

Jolene waved her away. "Let's do this."

We all sat up tall before Jolene pushed the magic button, making us live. "Welcome to *A Party of Two and the Wallflower*. Tonight, we have a special guest. Are you ready for this? Josh Keller, world-famous YouTuber, comedian, and social media sensation."

Josh patted his chest, pretending to be embarrassed by the introduction. But we all knew he loved every second.

"Woo-hoo," Tara hollered.

I said nothing as the wallflower.

"Welcome, Josh," Jolene offered.

He squeezed my leg. "It's great to be here and add to the party."

"Tonight, since it's Valentine's Day, we are talking about the perfect date ideas when you're an extrovert dating an introvert," Jolene informed the audience.

"Ooh," Tara chimed in.

"I'm an expert in this field," Josh bragged.

"Do tell," Tara egged him on.

Josh flashed me a dorky grin. "I just happen to be dating the most exquisite introvert on the planet."

Exquisite was a little much, but I would take it.

"So, what do you suggest?" Jolene asked. "Be warned, it must pass the test of our resident introvert. Do you want to say hi?"

"Hi," I said as blandly as possible, making my friends laugh.

"She's a tough nut to crack," Jolene warned Josh.

"I'm not worried."

"Okay." Tara wasn't convinced. "Lay it on us. Give us your best ideas for the perfect introverted Valentine's Day date."

Josh's eyes roved over me way too seductively for a semipublic setting. "First," he crooned, "we would start with the appropriate mood music while we cook her favorite meal together. Next," he said lowly, "while the food is in the oven, we would make some heat of our own while we danced, flush against each other."

Tara fanned herself. "Dang. Sign me up."

My cheeks pinked, thinking of how much I hoped he was giving me a preview of what would happen later tonight.

"I'm not finished yet." Josh's eyes owned me. "After dinner, I would pour her favorite drink and join her by the fire, where I would read her favorite book to her until it consumed her with such passion, she couldn't keep her hands off me."

"Mmm. Mmm," Jolene said, as if she'd just had the best meal of her life.

Josh, pleased with himself and the obvious blush that had overtaken my body, leaned closer to me but where the mic would still catch his voice. "What does our introvert think of that?"

I swallowed down all the inappropriate words I wanted to say and squeaked out, "Which book would you read to her?"

That burst the seductive air in the room as everyone busted out laughing.

"We told you she's a tough one," Tara roared.

Believe me, Josh had me at making dinner alone at home.

Josh wasn't deterred. "To answer your question, it would be *Anna Karenina* or *Rebecca*."

Oh, baby, take me now. I meant, "Excellent choices," I praised him. I was happy he remembered my favorites.

"Would you look at that?" Jolene said. "You impressed our wallflower."

"Any other advice for dating an introvert?"

Josh's hand inched up my thigh. "Don't be afraid to make the first move and always be willing to compromise."

"Do you agree?" Tara asked me.

"I certainly would never make a first move."

More laughter ensued.

"Good job, Josh," Jolene commended him. "I think we are all impressed."

Tara zeroed in on me. "I have a question for our wallflower. How would you plan the perfect date for an extrovert?"

Josh gave me his full attention.

I wasn't sure I could top his date. But that wasn't the point. I knew what Tara was asking. That being, how did we give and take in our relationship? I never wanted it to be one-sided.

I cleared my throat. "Well, first I would probably hyperventilate a bit and do some meditation."

Lots of snickering ensued because they knew it was true.

"After that, I would take him to a show or concert he really wanted to see. Of course, I would hold his hand the entire time and never leave his sight."

Josh's smile said he approved.

"Afterward, I would sing in the car with him because I know how much it would mean to him." My voice cracked a bit.

Josh gave me such a look of adoration.

There was a brief bit of silence as my best friends sat stunned, knowing exactly how hard that would be for me.

"What do you think about that date, Josh?" Tara asked.

"Absolute perfection," he responded before mouthing, "I love you."

Jolene interrupted the sweet moment. "Well, moving on now to a Valentine's Day edition of Smash or Pass."

I hid my groan. My best friends loved this. It was basically a game of which celebrity you would hook up with. My answer was always none of them. One time I even brought up a study about the myths of hookup culture and how really most women and men wanted stable, loving, monogamous relationships. We got a lot of comments agreeing, wishing society didn't put such pressure on people to quote, unquote hook up. Regardless, Jolene and Tara loved fantasizing about which famous men they would ravish if given the opportunity.

"We're going to change it up a bit since it's the day of love and ask if you would marry said celebrity. Are you ready?"

I definitely was. I was going to pass on each one.

"Here we go: Tom Holland."

"Marry," Tara was quick to say.

"Pass," for me.

"Hmm," Josh contemplated. "That's a tough one." Josh was so goofy. "If he's in the spidey suit, I'd totally put a ring on it."

We all giggled.

"I think I'm going to have to pass," Jolene agreed with me. "I need a bigger guy. Up next: Ryan Reynolds."

"Oh, baby, totally walking down the aisle," Tara said.

"Definitely," Jolene agreed.

Josh raised his hand. "Count me in."

"He's very married. Pass." I was always the Debbie Downer.

We did a few more rounds. And then . . . Jolene flashed me a devious grin before she said, "Our last celebrity of the night is . . . Josh Keller. I think we are going to let our wallflower answer first."

All eyes landed on me, but it was Josh's that I peered into, my heart beating out of control. His deep-chocolate eyes, boring into me, said this wasn't a game to him. "What's your answer?" he pleaded.

"Josh," I whispered, gripping his hand on my thigh.

"Yes," he said sexily.

Love Rescheduled

Everyone was going to know my identity after this. I had a feeling it was all part of the plan. Yes, this was well-orchestrated—that I knew. It had Josh written all over it. I also knew being with Josh wouldn't allow me to stay hidden in the shadows forever. I was kind of tired of hiding anyway. But . . . he deserved to sweat a bit for this little ruse he had cooked up with my best friends. He was obviously tired of waiting for me to ask for the ring. Oh, I was going to ask for it all right.

"It all depends on what the ring looks like," I called his bluff. Surely he didn't have it on him.

His face broke out in the hugest Cheshire grin as he let go of my hand and reached into his jeans pocket.

Blast him. I should have known he would be one step ahead of me.

He pulled out the most gorgeous vintage Arles diamond ring I had ever seen. It was elegant and not flashy in the least bit. Perfect for the introvert in his life. He held it up between us.

I stared, mesmerized by it, by him. A lump in my throat swelled. He'd carried the ring with him for over three years. He'd held on to me after I had pushed him away. The emotion of it all had me speechless.

"Natalie Archer. Oops, I wasn't supposed to use your name." He smirked.

My best friends thought it was hilarious.

"I hope you love this ring, because I love you. I know I was supposed to wait for you to ask for it, but I can't wait any longer. And the way I see it, we are way behind schedule as it is. So, please say you'll smash me. Marry me?"

I took off my headphones and grabbed his cute face, so badly wanting to smash him. "I love you, Josh Keller. I would love to be your wife."

"Woo-hoo!" Tara and Jolene shouted.

Josh placed the ring on my finger before pressing a kiss to my lips. "You're going to kill me for this later, aren't you?"

"Oh yeah."

He laughed. "Totally worth it."

It was definitely worth the wait.

twenty-four

JOSH PLAYED WITH MY RING as he held my hand. We were traipsing through the middle of a field. The only light was from a few nearby homes. More like country manors. I hoped no one called the authorities on us. Josh promised me we weren't trespassing. It wasn't the romantic date I had envisioned for Valentine's Day, but Josh said to trust him.

"I still can't believe you asked me to marry you on the podcast." I leaned into him, freezing.

"It was pure genius. I got to surprise you, and your BFFs got to be a part of it."

"The traitors," I laughed.

"Admit it—you secretly loved it."

I shivered from the cold. "All I can say is, I love you."

Josh chuckled and kissed my head. "You said yes, so let's call it a win."

I waved my free hand around. "So, what are we calling this?"

Josh paused and looked around the open field of tall dead grass surrounded by rolling hills before searching my eyes. "Our future."

I tipped my head to the side. "Our future?" I questioned.

He ran an icy finger down my cheek. "I've been doing a little more than negotiating with Mikey while I've been here. I've been looking at land, too, and talking to an architect."

"Wow," I spoke as a breath, seeing where this was going.

"This could all be ours."

I looked at the gorgeous and expensive nearby homes, each one on large plots like the one we were standing on. In my wildest dreams growing up, I never imagined living in such a place. Even less with such a man as Josh. Someone who loved me fully and completely, despite my quirks. Granted, I saw plenty of tiffs in our future. As long as we made up each time, that's all I cared about. "How much would all this cost?"

"We can afford it."

"You mean you can."

He drew me close and wrapped me in his arms. "No. I mean we."

I snuggled into him, soaking in the warmth of him and his words. "I should probably take on some more clients."

He laughed and stroked my hair. "If that's what you want, but it's unnecessary. I've been smart with *our* money. And we will continue to be. We can meet with the realtor and architect tomorrow if you'd like."

"You have been busy."

"Nat, I've been planning our future from the first moment I saw you."

I clung tighter to him, wondering how I ever got so lucky. "I suppose we better work on those plans, then. You know I love a good plan."

"I know that about you." He leaned back with an impish glint in his eye. "I was wondering if perhaps we could move up some of your plans."

"Which ones are those?"

"How dead set are you on getting married on September thirtieth?"

"Well . . . ," I exaggerated. "I already scheduled it on my calendar. You know how I feel about that."

His lips twitched before he went in for the kill, meaning his warm lips landed on my neck. Did he ever know how to nuzzle a neck . . . and get his way. He started with soft kisses before he ravaged my skin. Between his blissful assault, he whispered, "I'm more than tired of living away from you. And like I said earlier, we are way behind schedule. I think we need to remedy that. Like as soon as possible."

I tipped my head back to give him more playing room. "How soon are we talking?"

"How soon are you comfortable with?" It was the perfect response.

For a moment, I thought. "I would need a wedding gown, and Jolene and Tara are adamant on getting the perfect bridesmaids' dresses." I would probably need some time to hyperventilate a bit, but I would bring that up later, and I was sure Josh fully expected it. It was better not to ruin this moment—a perfect moment.

"Will that take seven months?"

"No," I laughed. I was a simple girl.

His head popped up. "So, what I'm hearing is, you *will* compromise on the wedding schedule."

There was that word again—*compromise*. Its use had both positive and negative connotations. But the wonderful thing about Josh is I knew he would never *compromise* my feelings, which made it easier to compromise with him. I knew there would still be times I had to tell that girl inside me it was okay to trust and know that just because we were letting go of the things we thought we needed to hide behind, it didn't mean we were unsafe. In fact, it opened the door to a kind of happy we had never known.

I gave him my best wicked smile, which was probably not wicked at all. "I think I could be willing, but tell me: What's in it for me?"

Josh gripped my jacket and brought us nose to nose. "I'll tell you what's in it for you . . . At least an hour of sexy time every day, toothpaste in the sink"—he grinned—"dirty underwear in various places around the house, loud rock music, lots of arguing and making up, and . . . a man that unequivocally believes you hung the moon and the stars."

"That's a very strong idiom."

He brushed my lips with his own. "I stand by every word."

I knew that. Truly, I did. So, what was I waiting for? A perfectly clean house with no one to share it with wasn't bringing me much joy. I missed Josh as much as he missed me. So, I checked with the girl inside me. Somehow, I could hear her say it was okay to make our dreams come true. She was counting on me. I couldn't let her down. She'd had enough of that in her lifetime.

"Let's get married." I took a deep breath in and let it out slowly, not believing what I was going to say next . . . "I'll let you pick the date."

Epilogue

Nine Months Later

JOSH PULLED ME ONTO HIS lap on the old couch in the dressing room at Laugh on Tap. He had refused to part with it when we did some minor updates and renovations that took a lot longer than we thought they would. "Hello, Mrs. Keller," he whispered low in my ear while he got very handsy. It was all part of his preshow ritual. I wasn't complaining.

"I hope you locked the door." I had at least insisted on that update.

"Yes, ma'am."

"Good." I grabbed his T-shirt and pulled him to my lips, drinking him in. I had gotten drunk a lot on him over the last nine months. Which meant I had some news for him. I'd been saving it for opening night. Laugh on Tap was reopening under new ownership—ours. I loved that word—*ours*.

"Mmm," Josh groaned, his tongue taking its time in my mouth, his hands driving my body like a back road.

"You have to go on soon, and our family and friends are waiting for us," I mumbled between kisses when he got exuberant, driving me wild. So wild it was going to lead to other things. Things which had led to . . . "And I have something I want to tell you."

That piqued Josh's interest. He tore his lips away from mine. "Everything okay?"

"Yes. I'm a little tired and nervous."

Josh blinked several times. "About the show tonight. You don't have to sit in the front row. I'm happy to have you backstage if that's more comfortable for you."

It was, but it was okay for me to be out of my comfort zone. I placed a finger to his aching-to-be-back-on-mine lips. "It's not that. I promised you I would be in the front row, and I meant it. I'm tired and nervous because, well, you can't keep your hands off me and all those extra hours of unscheduled sexy time have caught up to us, leading us to be way ahead of schedule." Like a full year ahead. I'd had it all planned out. We would be just settled in the new home we were having built with two master bathrooms, thank you very much. So much for that plan.

Josh's eyes went wide. "Are you trying to tell me you're pregnant?"

I nodded, hardly able to say the words. I'd been trying to digest it all since I'd taken the test last week. I should have probably told him before this moment, but I needed to process it first. It's not that I wasn't thrilled—I was. To know that a little piece of Josh and me was growing inside me was wonderful. My only wish was for the baby to be more of a neat freak like me, but I knew the odds were stacked against me. I had no doubt there was going to be a lot of toothpaste in my sinks for the rest of my life. It was worth the trade-off of going to sleep in Josh's arms every night. And I was hoping if I told Josh right before he went onstage, he wouldn't have time to come up with any jokes about impending fatherhood. I was hoping to keep it a secret for a while.

Tears formed in Josh's eyes before he planted a big kiss on me. "You just made me the happiest man alive. Holy hell, I'm going to be a dad." He looked me over. "Are you feeling okay? Can I get you anything?"

"The baby is the size of a poppy seed right now. I'm fine. Just a little tired."

"I'm here for you. Just say the word, and anything is yours."

"Just don't embarrass me tonight onstage."

"You mean I shouldn't mention the baby?" he teased.

"Don't you dare. I need to tell Jolene and Tara first, and your parents. And Alec and Hal and Stu."

Our life coach and our favorite old men were here for opening night. I loved "my guys" as I thought of them. I remembered back to our wedding day in April and how Alec had officiated. He'd made us promise to love, honor, and cherish each other as well as always call him every week. Hal and Stu were so honored to have walked me down the aisle in the cottage's backyard to a classical guitar instrumental of "Da Ya Think I'm Sexy." Yes, that was a compromise. It was a simple affair, but it was perfect for us. I'd even let Josh share some of our photos on his social media pages. He'd gotten a lot of mileage out of all the funny wedding videos he'd made making fun of bridal reveals. Jolene had starred in many of them with him. They were becoming quite the comedy duo. Both Camila and Josh had thought it best if they parted ways in that regard, considering their weird history and us getting back together. However, Camila and I had had some pleasant talks over the last few months. She was not the evil monster I had made her out to be. I learned that she and Josh had only come together because they were both nursing broken hearts and thought maybe their fans had been right: they *should* be in a relationship. But it only ended up being a way for them to hide their pain. She and her husband were also here tonight to support us.

"Fine," Josh agreed. "But get ready for a slew of videos making fun of gender reveals and ridiculous kid names. By the way, I love the sound of Josh Keller the second."

I rolled my eyes. "I will make a list of appropriate names to choose from, including meanings and popularity rankings."

He kissed my nose. "That's my girl."

"We better get out there before people think we're doing exactly what you want to be doing."

"Maybe we shouldn't disappoint them and do what they're thinking."

"I have the perfect hour scheduled for you later," I purred.

"I love it when you say that." He wriggled a hand under my blouse and rested it on my abdomen. "Thank you, Nat."

"For what?"

"This." He caressed my belly. "For you. For helping me make this night a reality."

"It's only fair I make your dreams come true as much as you've made mine."

He held me a little tighter. "I'm nowhere close to paying you back."

I loved that he thought so. Especially because I would be nagging him about his dirty underwear on the floor for eternity. "Let's go. I can't wait to see you onstage." I meant every word.

Josh groaned lowly into my ear, "I can't wait to get you home."

I snuggled in closer to him. "I am home."

If you enjoyed *Love Rescheduled,* here are some other books by Jennifer Peel that you may enjoy:

Christmas at Valentine Inn
The Valentine Inn
The Holiday Ex-Files
A Pumpkin and a Patch
All's Fair in Love and Blood
Love the One You're With
My Not So Wicked Stepbrother
Facial Recognition
The Sidelined Wife
How to Get Over Your Ex in Ninety Days
Narcissistic Tendencies
Trouble in Loveland
Paige's Turn

About the Author

Jennifer Peel is a *USA Today* bestselling author who didn't grow up wanting to be a writer—she was aiming for something more realistic, like being the first female president. When that didn't work out, she started writing just before her fortieth birthday. Now, after publishing several award-winning and bestselling novels, she's addicted to typing and chocolate. When she's not glued to her laptop and a bag of Dove dark chocolates, she loves spending time with her family, making daily Target runs, reading, and pretending she can do Zumba.

* * *

If you enjoyed this book, please rate and review it.
You can also connect with Jennifer on social media:
Facebook
Instagram
Pinterest

To learn more about Jennifer and her books, visit her website at www.jenniferpeel.com.